EXISTING

by

Dana Pride

Everlasting Publishing
Yakima, Washington
USA

Existing

Condensed excerpts from "My Mexican Summer 1975"
©1975, 1989 by April Diamond,
used by permission, were added later.

This is a work of fiction. Any resemblance to any
person, living or dead, is purely cioncidental.

Library of Congress Control Number
2006908762

ISBN: 0-9778083-2-7
ISBN-13: 978-0-9778083-2-8

First Edition
Everlasting Publishing
P.O. Box 1061
Yakima, WA 98907

EXISTING

For my family,
each who has encouraged me daily...

for those who know God has
a bigger and better plan
for our lives than we have...

and for everyone who needs to feel
the healing power of Jesus.

CHAPTER 1

"You can't say anything, not one word."

"Okay, I won't."

"Not a word!"

"Okay!"

"Promise!"

"I promise."

"Okay. Remember, you promised."

"Okay!"

Crystal looked into her sister's eyes to be sure she was telling the truth. Taylor didn't seem serious enough, but then what could she expect from a 12-year-old?

"And why can't we say anything?" Taylor asked.

"Because they don't really want us. They are just taking us because they have to."

"They don't have to. Mom said we were probably going to live with a foster family before she knew about them."

"They are like a foster family! And don't call her 'Mom!' If Tammy was really our mom, she would have kept us!"

"She couldn't keep us with all of her kids too. It was too many."

"You really listened to her, didn't you? We are just too different to stay with them. Well, that's why you can't talk to these guys, because they will just try to confuse you."

"You mean we can't EVER talk to them?"

"Never. You promised!"

"I know, I know! I won't."

"You girls need to put your seats in the upright position now, we're getting ready to land shortly," the flight attendant told them.

"Yes, ma'am," Taylor said, as she and Crystal obeyed.

This was the first time they had ever been on a plane. Crystal looked around so she could memorize the sights,

1

the sounds, the feel of the plane. She doubted they would ever have the opportunity to fly again. She was not looking forward to landing, and what would come after that; in fact, she was not looking forward to anything at all. What good could come out of flying across the country to live with people she couldn't remember, who didn't want them anyway?

"Maybe they'll be really nice," Taylor said.

"If they are, it's only because they have to be."

"No, they don't."

"Well, it doesn't matter. We don't have anything to say to them."

"How will we know them?"

"I think Mo—Tammy sent them a picture of us."

"But why would they take us if they don't have to? They're not relatives or anything."

"I don't know why, but do you really think anyone would want us? Look at us! Everyone on this plane is white, and we are mixed."

"Daddy always said we were golden brown."

"I told you not to talk about him!"

"But I--"

"Not a word! The plane is about to land."

The girls were silent for the rest of the flight. This was how Crystal liked it – silent. She didn't want to explain anything to anybody and she didn't want to hear what anyone else had to say about anything. Nobody knew her, what was inside of her, and nobody wanted to know. Nobody cared, and she didn't need anybody bothering her.

The plane landed in Portland, Oregon. Crystal and Taylor got their bags from the overhead bin and followed the other passengers into the airport. While Taylor looked around curiously, Crystal kept her head down to avoid the stares of the strangers.

"Hello, girls," a friendly voice boomed enthusiastically. "Welcome to the Great Northwest!"

Crystal tapped Taylor to remind her not to say anything. Taylor nodded, as Crystal glanced up and then away from the man with the friendly voice. She caught a glimpse of a big smile and gentle eyes.

"You must be tired after that long flight," he continued. "You probably don't remember me and my wife, but we remember you. I'm Pastor Young, and this is my wife, Sister Young. You girls have really grown!"

"Well, it has been 10 years – or was it 11?" Sister Young said kindly. Crystal didn't remember them at all. She was surprised to see that they were a mixed couple; Pastor Young was black and his wife was white. That might explain why she and Taylor were being transported across the country to live with them; but that still didn't mean they wanted Crystal and Taylor. Crystal avoided their eyes.

"Do you have a suitcase? Did you check any luggage?" Pastor Young asked.

Taylor shook her head and held up her paper sack with her clothes in it. They hadn't been able to bring much; they hadn't had much to bring. Crystal didn't respond.

"Well, let's go to the car," Pastor Young said. "We have a long drive ahead of us. Are you girls hungry?"

Crystal didn't feel hungry. She looked at Taylor, who glared at her and frowned, without responding verbally.

"I'm sure you must be, after that long flight," Sister Young said. "We'll get something to go, and you can eat it in the car."

"Do you like hamburgers?" Pastor Young asked. Without waiting for an answer, he continued, "Or do you like chicken? We'll pick up some chicken. I'm a little hungry myself."

Pastor Young continued to talk as they walked across the huge airport and through the parking garage to the car. It wasn't a new car, but it was a pretty turquoise color, and it was very clean. Pastor Young opened the door for them to get in the back seat.

"It will be nice to have young people in the house again," Sister Young remarked. "And girls! We've only had boys before. I am really happy you are coming to live with us. I think you're going to like our home. We live on a farm – did your mother tell you? -- way out in the country, and we have plenty of room."

Crystal was familiar with farm life in Tennessee. They had lived on the edge of a small town, on a dusty farm. The kids at school had teased them – not so much for being poor, because they all were poor, but because she and Taylor were the only two people in town who didn't have blond hair. The other kids had called them awful names and most of them wouldn't even speak to Crystal. It had become easy for her not to talk to people, especially during the past few months. Taylor had had a couple of friends at school but Crystal was sure they wouldn't last long, as soon as they were old enough to realize how different she was from everybody else in that small town.

Crystal looked with disinterest out the car window to the lights of the city as they drove away from the airport. She couldn't remember ever being in a city this big, a city full of selfish, stuck-up people who didn't care anything about anyone but themselves. She tuned out the conversation that Pastor Young and his wife were attempting to have with her and Taylor. The lights became a blur and Crystal fell into a deep sleep before they stopped to get the chicken.

CHAPTER 2

Crystal opened her eyes in an unfamiliar room. Was she dreaming? The room was warm and large, and the walls were painted a deep rose pink, with a colorful, flowered border near the ceiling. She turned her head to see the same flower pattern on the curtains and comforters, then she saw Taylor sleeping in a bed across from her. She sat up, remembering the flight and realizing where she was. A large, wood dresser with a big mirror matched a tall dresser and two night stands. A big closet was on the other side of Taylor's bed, and two doors led... where? She struggled to remember how she got here, but to no avail. She knew they were at Pastor Young's farm, but where was that?

She quietly got out of the bed and saw that she was still dressed in her traveling clothes. She touched Taylor on the arm.

"What?" Taylor asked.

"Shhh! They'll hear you!" Crystal whispered.

"Who?"

"Be quiet, you promised!"

"Oh, that," Taylor mumbled and rolled over.

"Do you know where we are?" Crystal asked, still whispering.

"Yeah, we're at Pastor Young's farm."

"I know, but where?"

"Somewhere way out in the country. We were both asleep when we got here, so he carried us in and Sister Young tucked us in our beds."

"How do you know, if we were both asleep?"

"I woke up in the car a couple of times, and then I started to wake up when he was carrying me, but then I saw that everything was all right, so I let them take care of us and I went back to sleep."

Crystal heard singing in the hall and scrambled back into the bed and covered herself. The door opened slightly and Sister Young peeked in.

"Good morning, girls!" she said with a smile, flowing into the room. "I see you are awake! You must have been so tired. Oh, and I'm sure you'll need to use the bathroom soon – it's right through that door. Are you ready for some breakfast? You were both fast asleep by the time we stopped to get the chicken last night, and we didn't want to wake you. You need a good breakfast to get you started on your day. Well, take your time, and feel free to look around inside the house, and after we eat we'll show you around the property, and you can meet the animals. Do you like animals? Have you ever seen a llama?"

Crystal could see that Taylor wanted to respond – she loved animals – but Crystal's stern glance stopped her. None of it really mattered to Crystal; as a matter of fact, nothing mattered at all. As far as she was concerned, she and her sister had been removed from one existence and into another, but nothing had changed. They were still unwanted and unloved, and life had nothing to offer them.

"Every morning, before we start our day, Pastor Young and I get on our knees and hold hands and pray together. Do you girls pray? I know you're from a good Christian family," Sister Young said. She didn't seem bothered when they didn't answer, she just continued talking to them in her compassionate manner. "I know this is hard for you, coming to a strange place to live with strange people, but you will find that we are not that strange, and even for what you might think are old people, we still have fun. Actually, we are not that old, but I know how we look to young people. I was young once, not that long ago, and I thought anyone over thirty was ancient. But we still ride bikes, play with our pets, I love to roller skate, and in the winter we have fun in the snow. Did you have snow where you lived in Tennessee?" She waited for a second for a reply and when she didn't get one, she continued, "We get some snow here in the winter, because we are up in the mountains. When we go outside, you'll be able to see where we are. But now that it's summer, we probably won't even see any rain for a few months. Oh, here I am, going on and on, and you need to get ready for breakfast. We have plenty of time to talk and to get to know each other. If you want to take a shower, go ahead. Clean towels are hanging on the racks. That is your bathroom, just for the two of you. Oh, and if you want separate bedrooms, we have plenty of room, just let me know. We put you both in the same room last night so you wouldn't wake up alone in a new place. Follow your noses when you smell the bacon!" she said cheerily, as she left the room.

Crystal wondered just how old Sister Young was, and why she was called Sister Young instead of Mrs. Young, or by her first name, whatever it was. Was she a nun? No, nuns couldn't be married, or could they? Well, it really didn't matter, and it wasn't important. Nothing was important. Crystal pulled herself up and went into the bathroom, a large room, painted bright yellow, with turquoise towels and rugs. It had another door – was it a closet? She opened it just a crack and saw an adjoining bedroom on the other side, this one also large and painted a lavender color, with deep purple curtains and comforters. Just the two rooms she had seen were larger than their whole house back in Tennessee, the house where 10 people had lived happily, just a few months ago. Now nobody could live happily, ever again.

Crystal washed her hands and face and returned to the bedroom where Taylor was changing her clothes.

"She is so nice, can't we just talk to her?" Taylor whispered.

"No! We don't need to talk to anyone. It won't make any difference," Crystal insisted.

"I want to talk to her."

"You promised."

Taylor didn't answer. Crystal took some clothes out of her paper sack and changed into them. The sisters left the room in silence and walked down the long hallway to the large, bright kitchen where Sister Young was preparing breakfast. Crystal didn't have much of an appetite, but she preferred to just go along with what was expected of her so people wouldn't bother her with questions.

Pastor Young was seated at a large table in the dining room. "Well, you girls look refreshed this morning!" he said cheerfully. "Did you sleep well?"

Taylor nodded, but Crystal didn't respond.

"I didn't hear you," Pastor Young said. "Did you sleep well?"

Taylor glanced at Crystal and nodded again.

"Well, okay. You'll find that we are talkers around here. We are 17 miles away from the nearest town, which is Goldendale, so we don't get much conversation during the day, except among ourselves. When people come by, you will notice that most of them are talkers too. It must have something to do with working out on a farm all day, being out in nature, and not sitting around talking on a job, like city folks do."

"Crystal, you can sit over there, and Taylor, you can sit across from her," Sister Young said. Crystal and Taylor joined Pastor Young at the table while Sister Young brought breakfast from the kitchen. The room was beautifully furnished; all the silverware matched, the plates and glasses had the same pattern and each place setting had a cloth napkin. The house was larger and nicer than any house Crystal had ever visited. The rooms were brightly lit with sun coming through the skylights in the living room and kitchen. She looked toward the living room where a sliding glass door and huge picture window revealed that the environment was the complete opposite of their farm in Tennessee. Outside were trees and hills as far as the eye could see, with so many shades of green everywhere. Crystal turned her head to look out another sliding glass door toward the back yard and saw thick green grass enclosed by a wood fence and a huge dog that looked like a horse! No, it was a small horse, the size of a large dog, who wandered over to the window and looked longingly at Sister Young.

"Mercury! It's not time for you to eat yet," Sister Young said. "Crystal, Taylor, meet Mercury, our miniature horse. He looks like he's just a colt or a pony, but he's a full grown horse. He's like part of the family. We have a pasture for him, but he likes to come in the back yard."

"He's Sister Young's baby," Pastor Young explained, "along with the four cats and the two llamas."

"And Pepe," Sister Young added.

"And Pepe," Pastor Young repeated, "her little dog. Most of the pets are hers, except Prince, our big dog. He's mine. See him out there, in that big dog house?" Crystal couldn't see him from where she was.

"He's about the same size as Mercury," Sister Young said, "and they act like they are brothers, a horse and a dog. They follow us all over the property."

"After we eat, we'll show you around the property," Pastor Young said. "God has blessed us with 40 acres, way out here, away from the city and the traffic and the noise."

"And away from the rush of people everywhere," Sister Young added. "It is so peaceful and quiet out here. The pace of life here is busy, but not hectic."

"We never run out of things to do," Pastor Young said. "Let us bless the table before we eat. Heavenly Father, we thank You for Your many blessings, and for providing for all of our needs. We thank You for these two young ladies coming to live with us and we thank You in advance for what You are going to do in their lives, this summer and for the rest of their lives. Thank You for the healing that is about to take place, that is taking place already in each of them. Touch those on our prayer list, in Jesus' name."

"O Lord, our Lord, how excellent is Thy name in all the earth! In Jesus' name we pray, amen," Sister Young added. "Help yourselves, girls. We have plenty of food."

"You must be hungry, since you didn't even stay awake for the chicken last night," Pastor Young said, passing a bowl of hash browns to Taylor.

Crystal looked at all the food on the table: scrambled eggs and hash browns and toast and jam and bacon and sausage, along with orange juice and milk. She still didn't feel hungry. She didn't feel anything. She watched Taylor take some of

9

everything. To avoid being questioned, Crystal politely took a small amount of eggs and a slice of toast.

"This is fresh squeezed orange juice," Sister Young said. "I just made it a few minutes ago." She poured some into Crystal's glass.

"And you have to taste this bacon," Pastor Young said. "It came from our neighbor, the butcher. He always has the best meat you can imagine, not like what you would get from the supermarket." He put two strips of bacon on each of the girls' plates.

Taylor began to eat heartily while Crystal sipped her juice, which was incredibly sweet. She nibbled at the food on her plate, which tasted good, but she didn't have the appetite to eat very much. She forced herself to eat a few bites, avoiding the eyes of Pastor and Sister Young. Taylor seemed to be ignoring her, or maybe she was just involved with her meal. Everyone finished eating without anyone making a fuss about all the food left on Crystal's plate. Sister Young began to gather up the dishes and take them to the kitchen. Taylor took her dishes to the sink while Crystal sat at the table, unfeeling, not motivated to do anything or even move.

"Come on, let me show you around the house," Pastor Young said. "As you can see, this is the dining room and kitchen, and we have a family room back through there, with a bathroom at the back. We can open all this up, and the living room too, when we have a big gathering," he said, sliding a portion of the wall back to reveal a large family room with several couches and a big TV. "The garage is through that door, and up here is the front door. It's not really a front door, but it's the main entrance for guests. We don't use it very often – I usually come through the garage or the downstairs door, and Sister Young goes in and out the back door most of the time, where her pets are."

Crystal and Taylor followed Pastor Young. The main entrance area was a small circular room with windows on one side and one large door and two smaller doors.

"That is the front door, this is a walk-in closet--" he

opened the door to show a closet as big as a small room, then he closed it and opened the third door "--and this goes to the stairs, up and down. We have a bonus room over the garage, which is really like an apartment in itself, with its own bathroom and mini-kitchen, and then we have a big storage room on the other side, with a stairway back down into the garage. You can explore the house on your own later." He led them back to the living room and Sister Young joined them. Crystal noticed a small area with a low wooden bench with a cushion on it connected to some kind of wooden bars and a big cross on the top of it. A couch and two chairs were facing it.

"That is our family altar," Pastor Young said. "Feel free to come and pray here any time you want to, or need to, day or night. That cushion is for kneeling."

"This house has four sliding glass doors," Sister Young said, "the one in the family room just off the kitchen, where you saw Mercury earlier, this one, one downstairs, and one in our bedroom. This balcony goes all the way across the front of the house, and we can see most of our property from it. But this is my favorite place," she said, leading them into a large round room next to the living room.

"This is our library," Pastor Young said, outstretching his hand, welcoming them to enter. The library had windows on one curved wall, and shelves and shelves of books on the other sides, or curved walls. A stairway curved up one wall to an indoor balcony and more shelves and windows, and another stairway. "We can go up that top stairway and go outside, onto the library roof. It's like a tower in a castle. We have a telescope we use to look at the stars. It's a little too hot outside to go up there now, but early in the morning or late in the evening we can see Mount Adams to the northwest and the hills in all directions. At night we go up there and we can see millions of stars, many, many more than you can see from the city, because we have no street lights out here."

"I really love the library, for one, because I love books, but I also love to sit in here and read or write or just look out the windows. Feel free to read any of the books in here. I only ask that when you take one out, if you don't know where you got it, just put it on the table and I'll put it away later. We have an organization system so we can easily find any specific book. Sometimes people borrow books, and when they do, we don't expect to get them back, and that's okay. What good are all these books if no one reads them?"

Crystal had loved to read, at one time, and she was a very good reader. However, now books didn't seem interesting. Even this room didn't seem interesting, and she had no desire to come in here, or be anywhere. She followed the others down the hall toward the bedrooms.

"We have three guest bedrooms on this side, a bathroom over here, and then the bathroom that's between those two bedrooms," Pastor Young explained. He opened the doors one by one and they looked in. Crystal saw the two bedrooms she had seen earlier, and one more that was similarly furnished and slightly larger.

"At the end of the hall is the laundry room, behind these doors." Pastor Young opened a door to reveal a washer and dryer and shelves of cleaning items.

"This is our room, and I have an office in here," Sister Young said. "Come on in, I want you to see how neat this is. I really love it."

They entered a very large bedroom painted dark turquoise, with lots of open space, more bookshelves built in the walls, three large dressers, a king sized bed that looked small in this huge room, two large closets, one which was a walk-in closet. Like in the living room and library, one whole wall was covered with windows and a sliding glass door. At the far end of the room sat a computer and chair, with two small file cabinets and more shelves of books, obviously Sister Young's office. An open door led to yet another circular room, this one sticking out of the house with frosted windows all around it.

"That's our hot tub in there," Sister Young said. "Actually, it's one of two hot tubs we have, this is the small one. We have another big one out in the back yard, big enough for about 10 people. Through this walk-in closet, we have our bathroom. You girls are welcome to come in our room any time the door is open, but if it is closed, please knock. Pastor Young doesn't sleep very much, but when he does, we don't want to disturb him."

"I have a 4 a.m. prayer hour," Pastor Young said, "and I go to the altar we saw in the living room, and then I usually just stay up after that. When I can, I get naps throughout the day. Let me show you my office now," he said, opening a door near the one where they had entered the bedroom to reveal a stairway going downstairs.

"We have three staircases leading downstairs: this one, which goes from our room to my office, and another one at each end of the house," Pastor Young said.

They went down a flight of stairs right into a large circular office beneath the library, again, with a wall of windows on one side. Several file cabinets, two desks, five chairs and one wall full of books on bookshelves gave the impression that this was an office where a lot was accomplished. "Through here is a bathroom, and if we go through it, we get to the exercise room." They walked through the bathroom, which had a shower and a small closet, and went into the exercise room. Several pieces of gym equipment sat on mats, and a mirror covered most of the far wall. A door led outside and Crystal could see that this was the ground floor. She figured the house must be on a hill, because the back yard was upstairs, but this part of the yard was downstairs. She followed the group out of the exercise room into the hall.

"Back here we have another bedroom and bathroom, and our storage rooms," Sister Young said, opening a door to reveal a huge room with many large shelves full of canned goods and other types of food and supplies, "where we store things and also food. In the winter, we get lots of snow and the temperature drops, so we make sure we are stocked up all year 'round. And we often have visitors and guests who are in need of a good meal, so we want to be sure we have enough to share."

"Over here is our meeting room," Pastor Young said, leading them into a large open area, which must have been directly under the living room and dining room. A large wood stove sat on the side of the room which shared the wall with the pastor's office. "Sometimes we have gatherings here, and sometimes we have barbeques out there." He opened a sliding glass door and took them outside to the front yard, which had a wood deck and a concrete patio with several picnic tables and benches, and a huge, bright green lawn.

"Pastor Young really knows how to barbeque," Sister Young said, smiling. She really seemed to care for her husband. "And somehow, the neighbors always know when he's fixing something, and they all just kind of drift this way. As you can see, our nearest neighbors are way over there, and way back there." The houses were so far away, Crystal didn't even consider those to be neighbors; it seemed as if each house lived in a neighborhood of its own, with acres and acres between them.

They walked to the edge of the lawn to admire the view. Crystal looked up at the house, which was now behind them. It looked almost like a castle with the three round 'tower' rooms, except it was made of logs instead of stone. The natural wood color gave a feeling of warmth to the house that a castle could never be capable of radiating. A covered balcony stretched across the entire front of the upstairs, and a smaller balcony was on the roof of the library. She saw two skylights, one over the living room and one over the master bedroom, but from this angle, she couldn't see the one over the kitchen. She noticed some odd rectangles with circles in them on the roof. The house was enormous, much bigger than any house Crystal had ever even seen. The house sat on the side of the hill overlooking the property and was surrounded by trees, with a big grassy front yard where they were standing. She gazed down the hill and saw several small cabins in one area, a group of trees planted in neat rows, and near the ponds, a round building that looked like it might be a church, with a lawn and trees near it. The green in this area was such a contrast to the dusty farm where they had lived in Tennessee, Crystal wondered how they could both be called farms when they were so different. Off to one side of the house were several fenced areas. Two llamas, a brown one and a black-and-white one, stood at attention in one of the fenced areas. They seemed to be watching her, leaning their necks over the top of the fence. She turned away from them. She didn't like animals, and she didn't like anyone to watch her. She didn't even like the outdoors. She didn't understand how Taylor could like animals or the outdoors, especially now, when nothing mattered.

The silence of the atmosphere rang in Crystal's ears. She could not hear a car, a plane, machinery, kids screaming, animals fighting, or anything at all. She realized they really were far away from civilization. She did not feel any type of reaction to this realization; she was neither afraid nor glad nor upset about the fact that they were out in the middle of nowhere with a couple of strangers who said they had known them when they were little. She followed the group as they went on a small trail down the hill, winding through evergreen trees of all sizes and varieties, and bushes and flowers that Crystal did not recognize. They walked past a pond, and she could see it was much larger than it had looked from the window of the house. A row of tall trees lined one end of the pond, with several other kinds of trees nearby. Millions of wildflowers were growing everywhere.

"Isn't this beautiful?" Pastor Young was saying. "Have you ever seen any place like this before?" He stopped and looked at the girls, as if expecting an answer. Crystal thought Taylor was going to say something, but she just bit her lip and looked down instead of responding. "You girls are mighty quiet," he remarked, but didn't press them for an answer.

"Whenever you get ready to talk to us, we're ready," Sister Young said patiently, smiling at them. Crystal avoided her eyes. She didn't want to be analyzed; she didn't want anybody to notice anything about her. She hadn't wanted the kids at school to look at her because they saw that she was different from them, with their smooth, blond hair and pale skin. They had teased her and called her awful names. She would shrink into a corner, trying to disappear, moving about quietly, avoiding eye contact with anyone, because that might lead to a conversation. When her teachers called on her, she answered softly, if at all. Once a counselor had called her into the office and asked if she had any problems at home. Crystal had wanted to tell her that everything at home was fine, but the kids at school were the problem, and she even felt some of the teachers looking down on her; but she knew the counselor was just trying to categorize her and label her, and then do some kind of intervention at her house. To avoid the interruption of her home life, which had been perfectly fine, she sat and said nothing. The counselor asked if she felt depressed, and she shook her head, knowing that that wasn't the problem at all; the problem was the people at school who were so mean to her and wouldn't leave her alone.

"Right over here is the chapel," Pastor Young said. Crystal looked up and saw the round building she had seen from the yard, also much bigger than it had appeared from up there. She turned back to see the house and was surprised at how far away from it they were, then she looked back at the chapel. The building was two stories high.

"We have Sunday services here, and Bible Studies on Wednesday nights, and sometimes we have revivals," Pastor Young said, opening the door, which wasn't locked. As they entered the foyer, Crystal felt a completely different atmosphere; calm, cool, with a different kind of quiet. "Let's join hands for a word of prayer," Pastor Young said, taking her hand and his wife's hand to form a circle. His large hand was warm and gentle, in contrast to Taylor's tiny, wiggly hand in her other hand. Although Crystal didn't like anyone to touch her, she didn't pull away. She closed her eyes.

"Sister Young, will you pray?" Pastor Young said.

"Dear heavenly Father, we thank You for bringing us together in Your house. Thank You for these two girls who You have brought into our lives. Help us to be what You would want us to be. Let Your will be done, now and forever. In Jesus' name we pray, amen."

"Amen," Pastor Young said, releasing Crystal's hand. "Thank you, Sister Young, for that prayer. I want to show you around," he said to Crystal and Taylor. He opened a door in front of them.

"This is the sanctuary," he said softly. They entered a large, circular room with curved, dark brown pews around the sides and going up the walls, all facing the pulpit area. They stood silently for a moment. A deep blue carpet covered the floor. Crystal thought at least 300 people could easily fit in here, and wondered if that many people from around the area would come so far just to go to church. She followed the tour group out of the sanctuary to the hallway, which had closed doors on each side.

"We have offices and meeting rooms and classrooms all around the outer perimeter of the building," Sister Young explained, as Pastor Young opened the first door. "This is the church office, so when people first arrive, they can come in here and take care of business or get information, or whatever they need to do. Sometimes our church secretary, Sister Franklin, is here, making copies or answering the phone or just taking care of church business. You're going to love her, she is really sweet, just lives a couple of miles down the road." Crystal doubted that she would love her, because she didn't love anyone except Taylor, but she didn't voice her objection.

"And we have Sunday school classes around here," Pastor Young said, opening the next door to reveal a small classroom with a huge chalk board and lots of brightly colored papers tacked to a bulletin board. A rainbow with a cross coming out of it was painted on one wall. "This will be your classroom, Taylor," he said, "and it opens up into the next room, the teen room, when the two classes want to get together to show a movie or have a group project." He pulled back a room divider and Crystal saw another similar classroom, this one with a large mural of Jesus, standing with outstretched hands on a grassy hillside, covering one of the walls. The bulletin

17

board held announcements of teen events. A door led outside, and a split door led to the next room, in addition to the door to the hallway.

"This room is for the little kids," Pastor Young said, opening the door. Shelves of books and coloring supplies surrounded the tiny, colorful tables and chairs. One wall had a large chalkboard down low enough for young kids to reach. Another split door led to the next room.

"This is our nursery. Some of our teenagers like to take care of the babies," Sister Young explained, "and the other side opens up into the young women's classroom." The room was painted in pastel colors and had two cribs, a changing table, several rocking chairs, and some shelves with baby blankets and other baby supplies.

"We like all of our kids to be in the sanctuary during the Sunday service, but there are times when mothers need to use the nursery. Our sound system goes into every room, so wherever a person is inside the building, he or she can hear what is being said in the sanctuary," Pastor Young said, "but in the nursery, we can turn down the volume a little bit."

"Yeah, the speakers can get pretty loud," Sister Young said with a smile. Crystal wondered if she meant the speakers on the wall or the speakers who were speaking, but she didn't care enough to ask about it.

"That's a fact," Pastor Young agreed. "Here is the men's classroom," he said, briefly opening the door to show them, "and the restrooms are back here. Then we have the kitchen and fellowship area." He led them in through the kitchen, which was bright white and yellow, with sunflower towels and sunflower decorations everywhere, into a large dining room with a sliding glass door that led to a huge covered patio. A stack of tables was against one wall, with two racks of chairs beside them.

"Sometimes we have community dinners here, about once a month in the fall and winter," Sister Young said. "In the summer, we have community picnics on the holidays: Memorial Day, the Fourth of July and Labor Day, so get ready for a picnic soon, the Fourth of July is coming just around the corner. Everyone chips in to help, bringing food, setting up, serving the meal, cleaning up. Even though we are far away from the hub of a city, we really come together as a community out here, like they did in the old days. You are really going to love it. It's not like anything in the city."

Crystal wondered why Pastor Young and Sister Young kept insisting that they were going to love someone or something. They had no idea what she and Taylor would love, or if they could love anything. Well, when they realized what Crystal and Taylor were really like, maybe then they would just leave them alone and wouldn't bother with them any more.

"Then around the last corner, we have the Pastor's office," Sister Young said, opening the final door before they got back to the front foyer. The hallway had completely encircled the sanctuary. "We really like the way this church building is laid out, because people can go from room to room, all the way around, and not disturb the service inside the sanctuary. God has really blessed us with this place of worship."

"He gave us the plans," Pastor Young said. "The Lord told us how He wanted it to be built, and Sister Young drew up the plans from visions He had given to both of us. Then God sent willing workers who donated time and materials to build this church building. It was amazing to see the miracles He did while we were building, by sending just the right people when we needed them, all the contractors, the electricians, the painters, all right on time. That's what God does."

Crystal thought about how God had not been on time for her at all this year. He had left her on her own, to take care of her little sister, stripping her of everything that had been important to her. She couldn't think of anything good God had done for her, nothing good at all.

As they walked outside, Crystal blinked against the harsh brightness. The sun was directly above them, and the sky was cloudless. She did not like being outside in this kind of weather because she tanned so easily, and she was already so much darker than almost everyone she knew – except Pastor Young. He and Sister Young didn't seem to notice that their skin colors were very different.

"Over there is a parking lot for when people come to church," Sister Young said, "and see that asphalt path just beyond it? That path goes all the way around the edge of this 40-acre section of our property. We usually ride our bikes around it at least once every day, and sometimes I skate around it too. It is so fun to just go around the whole property – and then from the top end, you can look over into our back 40 acres, which is completely undeveloped, where the deer and other animals live. Do you girls like to ride bikes? We have a bunch of them in the garage, left over from all the boys we've raised."

"Let's go over to the other side before we show them the top end," Pastor Young said. "Over here, in that little valley at the bottom of that hill, we have cabins that we had built for homeless families, so they can always have a place to stay, away from whatever problems they may be facing in the city. Right now, no one lives there – a family just left last week, after God blessed them to get their own place. Families come here to get a new start, and they help with the farming. This is a fruit orchard here. We still have some ripe cherries on those trees over there, but the apples, peaches, pears, apricots and plums won't be ripe until August or September. See those pipes that look like tubes running through there? That's an irrigation system we built to water the trees. On that side over there is our vegetable garden with just about every vegetable you can imagine. We even have a big pumpkin patch where kids from all over the area come to pick out a pumpkin in the fall.

"Here are the cabins, and the road on this side is just over there, so if the people who come to live in the cabins have a job somewhere else, they can come and go easily without disturbing things on the rest of the property." Crystal could see the road that bordered two sides of the property. She was tired of walking and tired of listening, but she didn't show any signs of complaint. She just continued following the group. A slight breeze began to blow, and she heard an odd humming sound.

"Do you hear that?" Pastor Young asked. "That's the sound of the windmills we have across the top of the hill on that side," he said, pointing. "This entire farm is run by renewable resources – solar power and wind power. On the roof of each building are solar panels that convert the sun's light into energy, and then the windmills catch the wind and do the same thing. We have our own wells, too, for our water, and God has blessed us with an underground spring running right across our property, about 60 to 75 feet deep. That's where the ponds come from. They are deep in the spring and early summer, and then get shallow and sometimes just about dry in late fall, but we never run out of water, because of the underground spring."

"We also practice conservation," Sister Young added. "We don't waste as much as people in the city tend to do, because resources aren't as readily available. We have all we need, but we don't waste what we have."

They climbed a hill and followed a trail that gradually led them up to the back yard of the house. The little horse and a little black dog ran to the edge of the fence to greet them. The dog squeezed and wiggled through the gate and ran to Sister Young and leaped into her arms.

"Pepe! This is Pepe," Sister Young said. "Pepe, meet Crystal and Taylor." The little dog seemed to smile at them. Crystal had never seen a dog like that, with curly black hair like a poodle's, and white eyebrows. He was a fat little dog, not at all poodle-shaped. However, the unknown breed of dog wasn't enough to force her to speak to these people. Sister Young went over to Mercury and petted his head with her free hand, while still holding Pepe.

"Do you want to go and see the top end now, or would you rather wait until later?" Pastor Young asked. "Well, you're probably tired," he observed, "and I have some work to do. Why don't you just relax for awhile?" he suggested.

"Come on, girls, let's go inside," Sister Young said, opening the back gate and putting Pepe on the ground. Pepe seemed to be glued to her feet with rubber cement, bouncing and bobbing with Sister Young's every step. "You can meet the llamas later," she said. "We need to make a plan to go to the city and get you two some more clothes, maybe tomorrow or Thursday."

Ordinarily, Crystal would have loved to go shopping. It had been a rare treat, with Daddy and Taylor. However, nothing was ordinary any more and she didn't care if she had any new clothes or not. She really just wanted to be alone and get away from these bubbly people who didn't know how to be quiet.

"Are you about ready for some lunch? I made some bread this morning and it should be almost done by now," Sister Young said. "Oh, it's still early, and you had a late breakfast. You're probably not hungry yet." Neither Crystal nor Taylor responded in any way, so Sister Young kept talking.

"You girls have grown up to be such lovely young ladies, with such a sweet spirit. When you lived across the street from us in Vancouver, Taylor, you were just one, and Crystal, you were just three or four. Oh, that's right, you had your birthday, and you turned four, and Murray was seven. You had a big dog named... what was his name? Oh, yeah, Max, that was it, and you both loved him so much, and he let you dress him up and brush his long hair and do just about anything to him. You were so cute, your mom always did your hair in the cutest little braids and dressed you in little matching dresses. Crystal, you always were shy, but Taylor, you were so talkative, even when you were just a year old. I'm sure you don't remember that, though; you probably don't remember us at all."

Crystal strained to remember anything about what Sister Young had just said. What did she mean? Sister Young knew their mom? Their real mom didn't want them so she had left them with Daddy just after Taylor was born... hadn't she? Crystal and Taylor and Daddy had always lived in

Tennessee... hadn't they? Who was Murray, and why was that name familiar and comforting, like a word that had rolled off the back of her tongue, way, way back in her past, deep in her mind, a name that had made her laugh, and then cry when she could no longer speak it?

She noticed that the dining room wall was covered with photographs of people. Was it possible that the Youngs had a picture of Crystal's family, their neighbors of ten or more years ago? She tried to look at the pictures without looking like she was looking at them. She didn't want to seem interested in anything in this house, because she didn't want anybody probing into her mind, trying to 'fix' her. Nothing was wrong with her. She just didn't need anybody.

"Are you tired?" Sister Young asked. "Why don't you go and relax for awhile? You can watch TV in the family room – we have a satellite dish – or you can just rest in your room. I have a few things to do around the house. You are welcome to go anywhere in the house – but if you want to go outside, please let me know. I'll be in the back yard or here, in the kitchen."

The idea of television was not appealing to Crystal. She walked to the bedroom and flopped down on the bed. She needed some silence in her head. Things didn't quite make sense. Sister Young must have been mistaken about being their neighbors, unless she had lived in Tennessee too. They had never lived in Canada, Crystal was positive about that. What had Sister Young said about a dog? They had never had a dog. Tammy didn't like dogs, so they never had been able to have a dog.

Taylor joined her a few minutes later, closing the door behind her.

"What was she talking about?" Taylor whispered.

Crystal just shook her head, looking down at the bed.

"Aren't you even going to talk to me?" Taylor asked. "Are you going completely silent? Forever? I really want to talk to Sister Young, and ask her some questions. I didn't know we ever lived near them, I thought they just knew us

23

from Tennessee when we were little. Did we live in Canada? I thought we always lived in Tennessee." When Crystal didn't answer her, Taylor continued. "Who is Murray? I've never heard that name before, have you? Did we really have a dog? Crystal, if you're not going to talk to me, I'm going to ask Sister Young and find out what she was talking about."

"I don't know," Crystal whispered sharply. "She must be mistaken. We've always lived in Tennessee. And I don't know who Murray is."

"Let's go ask Sister Young."

"No! We can't talk to them!"

"Why not?"

"I already told you."

"But what if they do want us? They are a mixed couple, maybe they want mixed kids."

"No, they don't! They are just trying to be nice because they have to."

"They ARE being nice! And Sister Young is going to take us shopping for some new clothes."

"I don't want to go."

"Why not?"

"I don't feel like it."

"You don't feel like anything any more."

"Why should I?"

"Because, we're here, and this is our life now."

"So we should just go on like everything is normal, like nothing ever happened?"

"I just want to live," Taylor said, still whispering.

"We are living," Crystal said.

"But not like this. How can we shut them out when they are so nice to us?"

"How can we let them in, when they don't know us and they don't want us anyway?"

"But they do want us."

"No, they don't. You just can't tell, you're too young."

"You decided before we ever met them that they weren't going to like us. You didn't even give them a chance."

"I heard Tammy talking to them on the phone before we left, and I could tell by what she was saying that they didn't want us."

"How could you tell?"

"I could just tell."

"You're not being fair!"

"I'm not being fair? Life is not being fair to us!"

"What do you mean? We get to live in a house like a castle with some really nice people, a mixed couple who look like they could be our parents. Maybe they will be our parents. Maybe they'll adopt us."

"You are just a big dreamer. Wake up, Taylor, that is never going to happen."

"It could."

"No, it couldn't."

"Why not?"

"Because it just couldn't, okay? They don't even want us here."

"Well, we're here. Let's just enjoy it."

"How can we enjoy it?"

"Easy. There is a lot to enjoy here. Hey, did you see those three orange cats downstairs?"

"No, I didn't see them, and I am not going to enjoy it here. I don't like cats."

"How do you know? We've never had one."

"I just know, okay? Now leave me alone, I want to take a nap." If she went to sleep, she didn't have to think about everything, and things would be less confusing when she awakened, and then maybe Taylor would realize the truth about their situation.

"So you're saying that I can't go and talk to Sister Young?"

"Taylor! You promised!"

"Oh, all right. Maybe I'll take a nap too. This bed is pretty comfortable."

Crystal turned on her side, away from Taylor and closed her eyes. Murray, Murray, Murray, that name just kept ringing closer and closer to the front of her brain, but she could not place it. Just as she began to see an image of a boy who could be named Murray, she fell into a deep sleep.

CHAPTER 3

The sound of a yell awakened Crystal and she jerked up to a sitting position, startled, before she realized it had been her own voice. At first she didn't know where she was, in this brightly lit room; then she saw Taylor spring to her feet.

"What? What's the matter?" Taylor asked, climbing onto Crystal's bed to comfort her. "Did you have the dream again?"

"I almost made it in time, this time," Crystal said quietly, nodding.

"It was just a dream," Taylor said, getting close to her sister.

"I will never make it in time," Crystal said.

"You can't go back in time and do it over," Taylor said. "Even if you dream that you make it in time, it won't be real."

Crystal gazed at the pattern of the comforter on the bed. She knew Taylor was right. She could never go back and fix what had happened. She had arrived too late to save Daddy, and she would never be there on time.

The horrible scene replayed in her mind once again. Crystal could see it, hear it and feel it as if she were there again. She and Taylor had just gone to bed, and Crystal heard Daddy come into the house. He and Tammy and her kids had been gone all day to a family gathering at Tammy's parents' house, but Crystal and Taylor hadn't been invited, so they had stayed home. Normally, Daddy would've stayed home with them, but today was some kind of special day, so Tammy talked Daddy into going with them. Crystal knew the sound of her father's footsteps, so she knew it was him, and she could tell he was alone. She heard him moving around the house, and she waited for him; but he didn't come and say goodnight, and tell her and Taylor that they were his special angels, and give them both big hugs like he usually did every night. She heard him in the kitchen, going out to the garage and coming back in, then in the hall as he walked past their room without stopping to see them. She wanted to tell him goodnight and she wanted her hug, so she got out of bed. Just as she reached for the bedroom door knob, an explosion rang in her ears, shaking the entire house. Taylor jumped up out of bed, and they both scrambled to get out of the room. Crystal couldn't tell where the explosion had come from, so she began searching the house, with Taylor right behind her. She looked in Daddy's bedroom, and even though the light was off, she knew something was wrong in there. A sickening smell overwhelmed her. When she switched on the light, she saw Daddy's feet sticking out from the other side of the bed and blood splattered all over the wall behind the bed. She ran to him, pushing Taylor back, and then she saw the gun by Daddy's hand. His eyes were wide open and blood was all over him, running onto the floor around him. He seemed to be moving or trying to say something to her, so she moved up next to his face, her ears still ringing.

"Daddy? Daddy, what's the matter? What happened?" she asked, sobbing. He didn't move again. "Daddy!"

"Should I call 9-1-1?" Taylor asked.

"Yes! Call them right now!"

Taylor ran to the phone and Crystal could hear her saying something from a distance, as if from the far end of a tunnel. She felt her own heartbeat pounding in her ears before the blackness overtook her. When she woke up, she was lying on her own bed and Tammy was standing over her.

"Your daddy is dead," Tammy said softly. "Did he say anything to you when he came home?"

Crystal shook her head. Daddy hadn't said anything to her, and now she didn't want to say anything to Tammy, or to anyone else. If only she had gone to him when she first heard him, she could have stopped him. He had promised his daughters again and again that he would never leave them; so why did he? What had she done to make him do this to himself, and to them? Why didn't she run to him when he first got home? If she had, he would still be alive, and then her life wouldn't be ruined now. She must be a horrible daughter: first she drove her mother away, and now she had driven her father away too.

Everybody in their small town knew what had happened, but nobody talked about it. There was no funeral for Daddy. For the next few months, Crystal refused to talk to anyone but Taylor, and only when they were alone. Her silence wasn't really noticed at home, with all the other kids constantly talking. At school, the teachers and the kids didn't bother with her. No one forced her to talk. Near the end of May, just a few days before school was out for summer, Tammy told Crystal and Taylor that they were going to fly to Washington to live with Pastor Young and his wife. Tammy didn't ask them if they wanted to move, she just told them they were going. She had been nice to them when Daddy was alive, but after he died, she seemed to avoid them as much as she could. She was probably ashamed of them because they were mixed.

"It wasn't your fault," Taylor said.

"I could have stopped him."

"But you didn't know."

"I still should have stopped him."

"You couldn't!"

"Yes, I could have."

"But you can't do anything about it now."

Crystal couldn't say any more about it. She just shook her head.

"I'm hungry, are you?" Taylor asked.

"Not really."

"It must be dinner time, let's go see."

"You can go."

"Come on! You have to eat."

Crystal reluctantly followed Taylor to the dining room. Sister Young was in the kitchen.

"Hi, girls! Did you get a good rest? Are you hungry? Dinner is almost ready."

Taylor nodded, but Crystal merely stood there, unresponsive. Her gaze traveled to the photographs on the wall, and she stepped closer to them so she could see the faces of the people. She scanned each picture, looking for one with a family of four: a mother, a father and two little girls. Although she didn't see a family like the one she was seeking, she gradually became aware that all of the kids in these pictures were mixed. They were all photos of boys of various ages, some with Pastor Young and Sister Young.

"Oh, that's our family," Sister Young explained. "These are the boys that we've raised. Some were just toddlers when we got them, and some were teenagers. They all turned out to be fine boys, and we are proud of all of them. See the two boys in the corner, by the pond? That's Randall and Vance, they're twins. They are both in the Army now, and you are going to meet Randall's two boys next week. Randall's wife is bringing them over to stay with us for a few days. They are also twins, ten years old. Twins run in their family."

Crystal looked away from the photos. She didn't care about these people, and she didn't want a couple of little boys bugging her, especially boys whose mother didn't want them. She hoped they were the outdoor type who would stay outside and just leave her alone.

"Why don't you girls help me set the table? The napkins are over there, the silverware is in that drawer, and the plates and glasses are in the cupboard up there. Do you want milk to drink, or iced tea, or water?"

Taylor moved to help Sister Young while Crystal stood and gazed out the window. She saw that little horse in the back yard, playing with a big dog. What good was a little horse, anyway? Someone had to brush it and feed it and take care of it all the time, and what could it do? She wandered into the library while Taylor set the table for dinner. Crystal had no interest in the books, but the room was somehow soothing. The natural light from the wall of windows gave a feeling of being in an enclosed porch. Several comfortable chairs had been placed around the room. She stood in the middle of the room facing the windows and felt a sense of balance. She liked to be the only person in the middle of a room, the only person walking down the very center of a hallway or a sidewalk, with an equal amount of space on her left and on her right.

Her eyes followed the stairs up to the landing or balcony on the upper level, and she saw a window seat and some big, fluffy pillows that she hadn't noticed before: a cozy place to curl up with a book, for a person who might be interested in a book, she thought. She stood there staring, unmoving, for a few minutes, until a voice interrupted her.

"Everything is prepared for us," Pastor Young said. "Let's wash our hands and go eat."

Crystal went to the bathroom near her bedroom and washed her hands, then joined the others at the table. A steaming roasted chicken sat in the middle of the table, surrounded by dishes of mashed potatoes, gravy, green beans, corn and rolls. Each place setting had a green salad with tomatoes and a glass of milk. Taylor was looking from dish to dish, as if she were trying to decide where to start. Crystal sat in her chair and still didn't feel hungry.

"Let us join hands," Pastor Young said. "Father, for this food we are about to receive, we are truly thankful. Bless the hands that prepared it, and thank You for all You have done, all You are doing, and all You are going to do. In Jesus' mighty name we pray, amen. Doesn't everything look good? Thank you, Sister Young."

While the others began moving about, filling their plates, Crystal sat still. Everything seemed so pointless: God who was not listening, books when she didn't feel like reading, food when she didn't feel like eating, conversation when she didn't feel like talking, life when she didn't feel like living. She knew she couldn't take her own life, but she wished that she would just cease to exist. Even that wish was pointless, she knew, because she had been wishing it for months and it hadn't come true.

Pastor Young and Sister Young and Taylor had filled their plates and were eating.

"Help yourself, girls, we have plenty of food," Pastor Young said. Crystal thought about how cruel life was to her: when she had had an appetite, back in Tennessee when Daddy was alive, with all those kids in their house, there had never been enough food to satisfy her hunger. Now that she had no appetite, she was surrounded by an abundance of food. She took a roll and a little bit of chicken and began to pick at her salad.

"What kind of dressing do you want?" Sister Young asked. "We have Ranch, French, Thousand Island and Italian."

Crystal didn't respond.

"I didn't like dressing when I was a little girl," Sister Young said. "Whenever my family went to a restaurant to eat, which wasn't very often, the waitress would ask me what kind of dressing I wanted on my salad. I would say, 'No dressing,' and she would always ask, 'You want it *dry*?' I wanted it wet, not dry, but I was too shy to tell her that."

"You know, this table reminds me of a time when I was a boy," Pastor Young said. "I grew up in Tennessee, too, in Memphis. There were 11 of us in my family, six boys and three girls, and my mother and father. My dad worked two jobs, and down in the South at that time, African Americans didn't make much money. Still, God always provided for us. One year at Thanksgiving, my dad had been off work for a couple of weeks, so we didn't have but a little food in the kitchen. My dad told all of us to come to the kitchen and sit at the table to give thanks. We all looked at each other because there was nothing on the table, nothing cooking on the stove, but we knew better than to question Dad. We all held hands, and Dad prayed a prayer of thanksgiving. He prayed a long prayer, thanking the Lord for His many gifts, and for our Thanksgiving dinner. By the end of the prayer, it seemed like I could almost smell the turkey. We opened our eyes and I was surprised to see that nothing was on the table, because when Dad had prayed, I felt that God was answering his prayer. I started to get up from the table, and Dad told us to just sit for a few minutes, and for each of us to tell what we were thankful for. So we went around the table and we each told about something that we were thankful for, like our family, our friends, our home, our health, our school, our neighbors, our church and everything we could think of. We went on for about 45 minutes, each one of us remembering something else, and adding something else, and we were still thanking God when a knock came on the kitchen door." Pastor Young knocked on the table three times for emphasis.

"That was strange, because most people came to our front door, but this knock was on the back door, the kitchen door. Dad got up to see who it was, and there was a white lady we knew, she lived up on the hill, with three bags of groceries. She was a rich lady, but she was always nice to us. She said God had told her to bring us Thanksgiving dinner, so she did – and everything was already cooked and ready to eat, including a huge turkey, dressing, potatoes and gravy, greens, biscuits, macaroni and cheese, and even three sweet potato pies. My dad said, 'God is good,' and all of us kids shouted, 'All the time!' So we sat there and enjoyed the meal that God had prepared for us. In the Bible He promised that He'll never see the righteous forsaken nor His seed begging for bread."

"God always takes care of us," Sister Young said.

"He promised, and He always keeps his promise," Pastor Young said.

CHAPTER 4

Later, when Crystal and Taylor were in their room, Sister Young tapped lightly on the open door and asked, "Do you mind if I come in?" When they didn't answer, she came in and sat on the foot of Taylor's bed. "Are you girls doing all right?" she asked. Crystal looked at Taylor, to be sure she wasn't going to answer.

"I know this must be hard for you, coming to a new place to live with people you don't know. I'm sure these past few months have been difficult for both of you. Pastor Young and I knew your father very well. He was a good friend of ours. He was always so helpful, fixing things of ours that had broken, taking our dog for a walk, and just helping out in any way he could. When we heard that he had died, we were really upset. We really loved him. You know, when he took you girls to Tennessee, we thought we might never see any of you again. He called us often and he came back and visited us a couple of times, did you know that?" Crystal didn't know that. Neither of the girls answered.

Sister Young continued, "It's really hard to lose someone you love so much. I know your dad loved both of you, and he was so proud of you. He was always talking about you, how well you were doing in school, and we could see his love for you light up his face every time he talked about you.

"It is really sad when somebody you love so much dies; but you have to remember the good things about him. You keep him alive in your memory by thinking of him, by thinking of the good things, remembering the good times you had, the important things he said to you, the good things he said.

"We lost somebody very dear to us also. We lost our baby daughter. Pastor Young and I were so excited about having our first child together a couple of years after we got married. I was pregnant, and doing very well, and the baby was healthy and growing fast. One day a couple of months before she was due, although we didn't know she was a she at the time, I started feeling a lot of pain, contractions, and they started getting worse and worse. So we went to the hospital, and they told us the baby was about to be born. They said it was risky, but the baby had a good chance to survive, because she was already seven months old. Then the nurse left the room and suddenly I was having the baby. She was born before the nurse even got back to the room. She was a tiny baby and so beautiful. She looked just like her daddy, and she even had hair already. The nurse came in to check her, and then the doctor came in and checked her and checked me. Then a bunch of people were gathering around the bed and they let me hold her and I was surprised that they were letting me hold her. I was thinking that she should be in an incubator or something, and then they said there was a problem with her heart and she wasn't going to live very long.

"My heart was broken. I started crying when I thought about all the things I would never get to do with my daughter, all the things she would never get to do with me. As I held her, she just stopped breathing. She never cried, she never made a sound. Pastor Young mentioned that she was already in heaven. He reminded me that in the Bible, when David's son died, David said, 'he won't come back where I am, but I am going to go where he is.' And then Pastor Young gave me a scripture from Ephesians 6:10, which says, 'Be strong in the Lord and in the power of His might.'

"That didn't stop my mourning for our daughter. I didn't feel very strong. I still missed her so much and I felt like God was so far away from me. I wondered what I had done, because I was sure that it was my fault that she had died. I felt so guilty, like God was punishing me for some sin, and I didn't even know what it was. I believed in God, and I knew he had always been so good to me, and I wondered where He was then? Why had He done this to me? Why had He taken our baby away from us?

"We had chosen the name 'Joy' for a girl, but I didn't want to name her Joy, because I didn't see any association with joy and this baby. Then Pastor Young suggested we still name her Joy, because she went straight to heaven, where she lives in joy forever. Now when I think of her, I can picture her sitting on Jesus' lap, waiting for us in heaven.

"We had a memorial service for her a few days later, and I was surprised to see so many people at her memorial service – more than 50 people came, and none of them had even seen her. One of the mothers of the church saw that I was still hurting. She sat by me to comfort me, but nothing was helping me. I didn't feel God was with me. I just kept suffering, until she said to me, 'Just because you can't you feel God doesn't mean He's not there. He still is there, and He is still the same as He always was and always will be. He is still good, even if you don't feel it. He never changes.'

"When she told me that, it was like a big burden had been lifted from me. That memorial service turned out to be a healing service, not only for me, but also for other parents whose babies or children had died. We gave the people at the service a chance to talk, if they wanted to, not only to comfort us, but to comfort each other and themselves. One mother who had had a miscarriage years earlier said she had never had the opportunity to talk about the death of her baby. Because she hadn't told anyone she was pregnant, she didn't feel like she could tell anybody that her baby had died. One couple who had had a stillborn baby hadn't ever grieved over the death of their baby. One couple who had a baby who died when he was just a month old had never let themselves mourn. During this service, I felt my broken heart healing, and others did also.

"I realized that God had a plan for me, for us, a plan that wasn't like my plan, and that He really does care for me. The doctors told us that we couldn't have another baby, so we decided to become foster parents. We opened our home to those who needed a home. We took care of many kids temporarily when their parents were unable to keep them, for one reason or another. Sometimes the parents were in jail, sometimes they were on drugs, or were in drug treatment programs, or sometimes they just decided their children were too much for them to handle. We love each of those children as if they were our own, whether they lived with us for six months or sixteen years. The pictures that you saw in the dining room are of our 23 kids, which have all been boys, until now. You are the first girls we have had, and I am really happy about it. I love all of our boys, but really, every mother wants a little girl or two.

"I know it's hard for you to talk about your dad and what happened, but there comes a time when mourning needs to end and you need to move on with your life. The Bible tells us there's a time for all things, including a time to mourn, but it doesn't say that that's the only time we have. There are times when we should dance, times we should be silent, and also times when we should each speak. You have decided that now is a time to keep silent, and we respect that. We're not going to force you to talk to us. You don't have to say anything if you don't want to. But I really would like you to talk to me, so I can get to know you better. Nobody will ever replace your dad, just like nobody will ever replace our daughter; but God puts people together to help each other and to be what they need to each other.

"I know I've said a lot, but I just want to add one more thing. Have you heard the saying 'time heals all wounds?' Well, that's not really true. *God* heals all wounds. He is the only Healer. Let Him heal your broken hearts so you can begin to live again."

Crystal could feel Sister Young looking at her, but she refused to return her gaze. She stared at the bed, wondering why Sister Young was wasting her time talking to them. Nothing could help her, ever.

"I want to say a prayer for you and then I'll let you get to bed. Father, please let the healing process begin, and work a miracle in Crystal's and Taylor's hearts and in their lives, in Jesus' name, amen."

She stood up to leave, then stopped and turned to face them again. "If you want to read, feel free to help yourself to any of the books or magazines in the library. You can bring them in here, if you like, or read them anywhere you want. We don't have all those books just to decorate the shelves.

"Oh, one more thing. Let's go shopping on Friday. We'll go to one of the malls, it's about an hour away from here. Be thinking of what you need, like pajamas, shorts, summer clothes, swimming suits, underclothes, shoes, sandals. Sleep well. Good night."

As soon as they heard her walk down the hall, Taylor leaped across onto Crystal's bed.

"What are you doing?" Crystal whispered.

"I felt like jumping over here," Taylor whispered back. "Crystal, did you feel it? I feel my heart healing. I felt so sorry for Sister Young, but I know she really wants us. We have to talk to her."

"No, I don't feel anything. What was the point of her story, anyway? That everyone gets hurt and God hurts people who love Him?"

"No! That He cares for us and He wants us to feel better."

"Well, it doesn't work that way. I will never feel better."

"Maybe when we go shopping you'll feel better."

"I told you, I will never feel better. And you shouldn't either. What would Daddy think, if we suddenly got happy, like he wasn't even gone?"

"Do you think he would want us to be miserable all of our lives?"

"If he wanted us to be happy, he wouldn't have left us!"

"Well, he did leave us."

"And we are not happy, we can never be happy."

"Crystal, why do you keep saying never? We can never talk, we can never be happy. I want to talk. I want to be happy."

"We can't! Don't you understand? We just can't."

"No, I don't understand. I don't want to understand. I just want to get back to a normal life."

"We don't have a normal life, we never had a normal life, and we never will have a normal life."

"I think this is pretty close to normal."

"You are too young to understand."

"You are too old to care about my feelings!"

"Your feelings? What about my feelings?"

"It seems like you don't have any feelings anymore! You don't want to have any feelings! But you could if you wanted to. I do!"

Crystal didn't answer. Why did her sister have to know her so well? She refused to talk any more that evening and covered herself with her blanket. She didn't want to think about anything, not about the dinner or the baby that had died or how God had healed people when they were hurting. Crystal wasn't hurting: she didn't feel anything at all.

CHAPTER 5

The next morning, Crystal awakened to the smell of bacon. She immediately remembered where she was, and she didn't feel like getting out of bed. She imagined lying in bed all day, and when Sister Young would come in to see what was wrong, she would just not say anything. Then she imagined Sister Young calling a doctor, or worse, a counselor, to come and talk to her and tell her 'it's normal to be depressed in a situation like this.' She wasn't depressed, and she didn't want anyone to come and make a big deal out of nothing, so she got out of bed and got dressed. Taylor had already left the room, and Crystal hoped she hadn't broken her promise. They just didn't need people asking them questions and trying to find out what was going on inside of them. They just needed to be left alone, and then they would be fine. She went into the kitchen.

"Good morning, Crystal," Sister Young said cheerfully. Crystal didn't like that expression, because nothing was good any more. She wondered how long it would take before Sister Young stopped trying to be cheerful around her, before she realized it was a waste of her cheer. "Breakfast is just about ready, and Taylor is outside with Pastor Young. Some of our neighbors came by to help in the orchards, so they all went down there early this morning, while it was still cool. It's pretty warm outside now, even though we can't feel it in here. We don't have air conditioning, but the house is so well insulated and built to withstand any kind of weather, hot or cold. That is why most of our doors have entry ways; we don't just open a door to the outside, we open it to a type of buffer zone. And we have special windows that keep the outside weather outside of the house.

"Did you see the towels in your bathroom? Those are all clean, for you and Taylor to use. If you need another one, or a washcloth, look in the closet or in a drawer under the sink. You should have everything you need in there, shampoo, conditioner, body wash, lotion, but if you need anything that you don't see in there, just let me know and I'll get it for you. We probably have everything you'll need in our storage room, downstairs. We always stock up when we go to town, since we don't go very often."

Crystal did not find Sister Young to be interesting at all, but she supposed the information was useful. Sister Young was slicing some fruit on a cutting board, on the counter that faced into the dining room.

"My grandfather had a saying," Sister Young said, "and that was 'Always cut from you, you'll never get cut.' That is true, you know. As long as you are cutting away from your body, you won't cut yourself. My mother taught me that saying when I was about Taylor's age and just starting to learn to use a knife in the kitchen."

Always shoot from you, you'll never get shot, Crystal thought.

After breakfast, Pastor Young wanted to show Crystal and Taylor the rest of the property, what he called the 'top end' and the 'back 40.' They went through the garage, which was an enormous, 4-car garage with a workshop at one end, near the back side of the house. They had a small car, a bigger car and a sports utility vehicle in the garage, along with about 15 bicycles and a variety of fishing poles, volleyballs, soccer balls, nets, rackets, roller blades, roller skates, ice skates, baseballs, bats and gloves and other sporting equipment. Shelves around the garage held items for car maintenance, including oil, anti-freeze, windshield-washer fluid, towels and rags. The familiar smell of a garage brought back memories of Daddy, who was always working on somebody's car in their garage at home. For just an instant, Crystal pictured him sliding out from beneath a car with his hands, face and hair black with grease. He smiled when he saw her and asked teasingly, "Do you want to give your dad a kiss now?" reaching out to her.

She almost smiled to herself: then she remembered where she was and why she was there. Pastor Young walked over to the collection of bikes.

"We have bikes of every size, so I'm sure we have one to fit you. You just have to pick the color you like. This reddish color one is mine, and Sister Young's is the turquoise one over there, and the rest have belonged to our kids. In the summer, the best time of day to ride is in the early morning or late evening, if it's not too hot. Sister Young and I took a ride this morning, all the way around the perimeter of the front 40 acres. It's a good way to get a look at our whole property, and get some fresh air and exercise at the same time. Those are Sister Young's roller skates, the purple ones, she likes to skate around the property too. We have some skates that would probably fit you, or some roller blades, if you prefer."

Crystal and Taylor hadn't had much of an opportunity to ride bikes at home in Tennessee, because they only had two bikes to share among the eight kids. The other kids were so aggressive, they usually got them first. Crystal followed Taylor and Pastor Young into his workshop, where he had tools, work benches, and tool chests, with various projects in progress.

"This is my shop," Pastor Young said. "If you need anything fixed, we can probably fix it right here. You might be asking yourselves, 'why does he have so many tools?' Well, you need the right tool for each job, whether it be a hammer or screwdriver or wrench, and then you need the right size, too. Right through here we have the gardening tools," he said, opening another door, "and right out here is our greenhouse, where we grow fruits and vegetables year-round. Do you like strawberries? It looks like we need to come back later and pick some, we have a lot of ripe ones!"

Crystal looked through the steamed-up windows at the rows and rows of growing plants as Pastor Young began to walk up a hill on a path into the woods. She and Taylor followed him to the top of the ridge, and they soon came to a clearing.

"Over that way are the windmills you often hear humming," Pastor Young explained. Crystal saw a row of large, steel poles with blades on them that didn't look anything like windmills she had seen in pictures. From where they were standing, Crystal could see the house, the church and the orchards below them, in the valley.

"Right down there is our barn. We take the animals inside when it gets really cold. Beside the barn, see that long building? That's for our farm equipment." It looked like a long garage with ten garage doors, and it had a row of tall trees behind it. "We have tractors and trailers and old trucks and a riding lawn mower, and all kinds of things for working in the gardens and orchards.

"You might ask how this all came about. Well, I'm glad you asked. This home was a dream of mine and Sister Young's years ago, and we bought the property and then began to design where we wanted the buildings, and where we were going to put the orchards and gardens and everything. Then God blessed us so that everything began falling into place. We had volunteers help us to build the church and plant trees and seeds, and to build the cabins for the homeless. We had a group of brothers that put up each cabin in about a week. God provided everything we needed, and then just recently, He gave us the back 40 acres too. We haven't done anything back there yet, it is still all undeveloped land. We can follow this trail through the woods and take a look," he said, leading them on the trail.

Most of the trees in the woods were unlike the trees Crystal had known. These were evergreens, but they were not at all like Christmas trees – these had clusters of long, spikey needles. Some were very tall, and some were young trees no taller than Crystal. There were some other kinds of trees also, and lots of plants and wild flowers growing all over the place.

As they came to the far edge of the woods, they stood overlooking a valley that to Crystal resembled a place where fairy tales were created. The valley was green and grassy, with unusual trees clustered near little ponds. Hundreds of colorful wildflowers were scattered everywhere, creating a random yet balanced pattern. The whole valley was surrounded by hills, which were covered with trees. Crystal could imagine fairies and other types of tiny people gathering near the ponds in the moonlight. She noticed a look of awe on Taylor's face, and knew she was thinking the same thing. This was the place that was mentioned in the stories they had read when they were younger; this was the setting for the stories they had created.

"Isn't it beautiful?" Pastor Young asked quietly, bringing Crystal back to the present. "God designed this – it is untouched by man. We haven't even walked through the valley yet. See those trails? They are deer trails. We have a lot of deer around here. Sometimes we can hear coyotes back here. The wild animals don't come onto the Front 40 very often, because of all the people and activity going on, but they come to the ponds back here. Oh, see the deer over there?"

A large deer and a small deer seemed to appear out of nowhere, standing near one of the ponds. Crystal realized they had probably been there all this time, camouflaged in their environment. As Pastor Young and Taylor began to follow the trail back through the woods, Crystal stood, transfixed, staring into the valley, at its beauty. She began to feel something inside of her: she quickly repressed it and turned to follow the others back to the house.

When they arrived, Sister Young was outside and appeared to be playing with the little dog and the little horse. They were romping around, and she was stopping to pet them and say something, then they began to romp again. She stopped romping as they approached, but continued laughing with her pets.

"So, did you enjoy the Back 40? Isn't it beautiful? I love it! It's like a magical place," Sister Young said, as soon as they were in hearing range. Pepe bounced around her, wanting to play some more. Mercury charged over to Sister Young, forcing his head into her hand so she would pet him.

"I think the girls love it as much as we do," Pastor Young said, speaking for them. Crystal didn't bother to correct him, to say that she didn't love anything. That would only start a discussion, which would be much worse than Pastor Young stating his impression of what she and Taylor felt.

"Well, girls, it looks like we'll have to postpone our shopping trip until next week," Sister Young said. "Rachel, our son Randall's wife, called, and she and the boys are coming today."

"Today?" Pastor Young asked. "I thought they were planning to come next week."

"Vance called her this morning and said he's on his way here. Randall hasn't been released for his vacation, or leave, or whatever they call it, so Vance wants to meet Rachel here."

"What time are they coming?"

"I guess Rachel and the boys will be here in a little while. Vance should be here by dinner time."

"You girls will have someone to play with," Pastor Young said. "Kenny and Keith are about your age," he said.

"The boys are a little younger. They are only 10," Sister Young said, "but they are so friendly, you will love them."

Crystal didn't care one way or the other if any kids came to visit. She had no interest in meeting anyone else, even if they were friendly. She was too old to play anyway. Taylor could play with them, as long as she didn't talk to them. Crystal stood and stared at the orchards while Pastor Young and Sister Young discussed Rachel and Randall and Vance. She tuned them out and let her mind go blank.

Pepe bounced over to her and snapped her out of her trance. She tensed up, not wanting the dog to touch her. Then the little horse began to follow Pepe and come toward her also.

"They like you, Crystal," Sister Young said. "You can pet them. They won't hurt you." Crystal stood, frozen, not afraid, but just not wanting to make contact with them. Taylor came over near her, kneeled down and fluffed up Pepe's fur around his face, then she stood up to pet Mercury'. She put her face into his mane. Crystal could tell that Taylor liked them. Crystal didn't want to have anything to do with them, or with anyone, for that matter.

"Is that Randall's car down there?" Sister Young asked,

looking down at the road where a car had just come around the corner. The car looked as small as a toy, it was so far away.

"It sure looks like it," Pastor Young said.

CHAPTER 6

In a few minutes, they were standing outside the garage on a big, paved parking area, greeting Rachel and Kenny and Keith. Crystal noticed that they were all mixed. They were all were the same color as she was, and they had black hair and dark brown eyes like she and Taylor had. Rachel's hair was a lot like her own, thick and silky. Kenny and Keith had curly hair and were dressed alike.

"So how come you don't say anything?" one of the twins asked Taylor after the introductions were made. Taylor didn't answer.

"Are you guys deaf or something?" he asked. Taylor shook her head.

"How could they hear you if they are deaf?" the other twin asked.

"Then why don't you talk?" the first twin asked.

"The girls are very shy," Sister Young said.

"Don't bother them, Kenny," Rachel said. "If you girls want to know how to tell them apart, just listen to them. Kenny is a little more obnoxious than Keith," she said.

"I am not!" Kenny said.

"Are too," his brother said.

"I am not, you are!"

"No, you are, don't you have any manners?"

"Manners-shmanners," Kenny said. "What do you know about manners anyway?"

"I know how to be polite."

"Do not!"

"Do too."

"You do not!"

"I do too."

"Boys! Stop!" their mother said.

"He does not," Kenny said.

"Yes, I do," Keith said.

"Boys, what did your mother say?" Pastor Young asked. "Is this how you treat your mother? Show her some respect.

You probably don't talk back to her like that when your daddy is home, do you?"

"No, sir," they said together.

"What are you going to tell your mother?" Pastor Young asked.

"We're sorry," they both said.

"And?"

"And we won't do it again."

"That's better."

"Thanks, Dad," Rachel said. "They always listen to you."

"And they should be listening to you, right boys?"

"Yes, sir," they answered.

"Grandpa, can we ride bikes?" Kenny asked.

"Go ahead, you know where they are. Just be sure to stay on the property."

"Yes, sir!" The boys ran to the garage and charged out a moment later on bikes. They quickly disappeared on one of the trails.

"Crystal and Taylor, you girls can go too," Sister Young said. Taylor looked as if she wanted to go, but shook her head after glancing at her sister.

"You can come inside with us, or you can stay outside and play," Sister Young told them, as she led Pepe and Mercury around to the back of the house with Rachel following.

"I'm going to finish up a project in my shop," Pastor Young said, heading into his workshop.

Crystal and Taylor went in the house. Taylor headed for the library, so Crystal followed her. Taylor began looking at the selection of books while Crystal silently climbed the steps to the second floor landing. She looked down at Taylor, who had selected a book and settled into an easy chair, and wondered what good could come out of reading. She sat on the cushion of the window seat and stared out the window.

She didn't know if she had fallen asleep or had just been staring – she hadn't been dreaming or daydreaming - when she heard Sister Young calling them to come to dinner. She saw Taylor sprawled on the floor with magazines all around her. She watched her stack them neatly and put them on a table. Crystal came down the steps and they walked together into the dining room, where the twins were already seated.

"Claire, can I help you with that?" Rachel asked. So that was Sister Young's first name, Claire, Crystal thought. She and Taylor sat across from the boys. Pastor Young sat at the head of the table, with Sister Young and Rachel on either side of him.

"Wait for the prayer!" one twin said to the other, as he was reaching for his milk.

"My throat is dry," the other twin said.

"Kenny," their mother warned.

"Let us pray," Pastor Young said, as they all joined hands. "Father, we thank You for bringing us together once again at this table. We pray for Randall and Vance. We thank You in advance for their safe return. For this food we are about to receive, and for the hands that prepared it, we thank You. In Jesus' name we pray, amen."

"Amen!" the boys repeated.

"Pass the pork chops!" Kenny said loudly.

"Please," Keith added.

"Please!" Kenny shouted.

"Indoor voices, boys," Rachel said, passing them each a pork chop.

"Grandma makes the best pork chops," Keith bragged.

"My grandma," Kenny said.

"Mine!"

"Mine!"

"Boys!" Rachel said.

"We are at the dinner table," Pastor Young reminded them. Crystal looked at the food, not hungry, took a little bit of everything that was passed to her and continued passing the dishes around the table.

"Aren't you guys going to say anything?" Kenny asked.

"Leave them alone," Keith said.

"You guys are just weird," Kenny commented.

"Kenny," his mother said.

"Well, they are! They just sit there and don't say anything."

"That's a blessing," his mother said. "It would be nice, if for a few minutes you didn't say anything."

"Hey, where's Uncle Vance?" Keith asked. "I thought he was coming for dinner."

"He called and said he'll be here in an hour or so," Sister Young said. "He told us to go ahead and eat without him."

"*Please* hand me the biscuits," Kenny said. Keith passed him the basket of biscuits.

"You're welcome," Keith said to his brother.

"No, you're welcome," Kenny said.

"No, you're welcome," Keith said.

"You're a well CONE."

"YOU'RE a well cone."

"You're welconian, you Draconian."

"You're a Draconian."

"No, you're a Draconian."

"No, you are."

"No, you are."

"You are."

"You are."

"Boys, stop it," their mother said. "Mind your manners and eat your dinner."

"Since you are identical twins, wouldn't you *both* be Draconians?" Taylor asked. Everyone at the table stopped chewing and looked at her. Crystal tried to give her the punishing eye, but Taylor wouldn't look in her direction. Crystal wondered what they would do, now that Taylor had broken her silence. Sister Young was the first to resume the conversation.

"That sounds logical. What do you think, boys? Wouldn't you both be Draconians?" she asked. To Crystal's surprise, Sister Young didn't turn the spotlight on Taylor.

"Oh, man!" Keith yelled.

"Man!" Kenny yelled louder.

"Boys, we're at the table," their mother said quietly. "Use your inside voices."

"We ARE the same. Whatever you say I am, you are," Keith said softly.

"No, you are," Kenny argued.

"We both are!" Keith insisted.

"You guys are exactly the same," Taylor agreed. "You look alike, you dress alike, and you talk just the same as each other."

"I don't want to be like him," Kenny said.

"Well, I don't want to be like you," Keith said.

"You're twins, okay? You can't do anything about it," Taylor said.

"I'm going to Photoshop you out of the family portrait," Kenny said.

"I'm going to Photoshop you out," Keith said.

"I'll Photoshop myself back in," Kenny said.

"I'll Photoshop myself back in," Keith said.

"Then I'll Photoshop you back out," Kenny said.

"Who could tell the difference, unless you're both Photoshopped out?" Taylor said. "You both look exactly the same," she reminded them.

"Thank you, Taylor," their mother said. "They seem to forget that sometimes."

"Oh, man," Kenny said.

"You're a man," Keith said.

"And you're not! You're a baby!"

"Boys! That's enough," their mother said sternly. "Now, I don't want to hear another word from either of you until you finish your dinner and are excused from the table."

"Yes, ma'am," they said in unison, as they eagerly resumed eating.

Although Crystal wasn't looking directly at them, she could see them out of the corner of her eye, squirming in their seats, poking at each other. She glanced sideways at them and saw them making faces at each other, as if one of them were looking in a mirror. They didn't seem to notice her at all. Taylor was eating her dinner as if nothing unusual had happened, as if she hadn't broken her promise. Well, Crystal knew *she* would never have a reason to say anything to any of these people, not ever.

After dinner, Taylor ran outside with the boys while Pastor Young, Sister Young and Rachel sat in the living room and talked. Crystal sneaked upstairs to the window seat in the library and looked out the window. She could see the llamas looking over the fence at Taylor and Kenny and Keith as they ran around the grassy part of the yard. Crystal scooted over, scraping her leg on something, then saw a small hinge on the window seat, behind the cushion. She stood up and lifted open part of the bench, revealing a compartment beneath it. At first, she thought it was empty, then she noticed something tucked away, over to one side, a book. She reached down and pulled it out. The cover was blue and blank. She turned it over, but it had no printing at all on the cover. She opened it and saw that it was hand-written. It looked like a dairy. She turned to the first page and began to read.

JULY 16, 1975--THE NIGHT BEFORE THE FIRST DAY

I'm so excited, tomorrow is the big day! Time for a change, time to do something different, time for fun and freedom and a new lifestyle! How can I possibly sleep? I've never been to Mexico, and tomorrow I am going for 5 weeks! Plus, I'll be getting college credit and I'm not even out of high school yet! Mom and Dad are letting me go with a group from the college, 2 instructors and 14 students. I met most of them once, at a meeting at the college. I hope this one girl I saw (Lisa?) will be my roommate. I didn't get a chance to talk to her, but she looked like the only person near my age. A tall, cute guy, who introduced himself to me as Bart, mentioned to me that he likes music, so I picked up a couple more cassettes for the trip. Of course, I'm taking my cassette recorder; well, actually, it's Jeremy's, because mine doesn't work, but Jeremy's letting me use his; he's a cool bro. Even though he's only 11, we are so much alike. We can always make a compromise, but he does get on my nerves sometimes. I won't have to see him for 5 weeks! (Yeah, I'll miss him a little.)

I know I should get to sleep, but who can sleep on a night like this? I went out driving around tonight (my last chance before this Big Trip) with Astra, my best friend, and Mike, the guy who currently likes me. (They say they'll miss me, ha!) Oh, well, (I'm not looking for romance on this trip, I want to get away from guys! Give me a break!) I'm going to have fun! Astra seemed sort of sad, like I'm going to forget her or forget she's my best friend. I'll never forget about her! Mike said he won't meet any new girls while I'm gone. Right. Well, I won't meet any new guys either; but I did tell him I need to be free. I just want to be one of the girls, one of the people, not half of a couple.

OK, I guess I'm ready to try to relax enough to fail asleep. I hear Jeremy in his room, but I think I can sleep through his noises. I won't hear them again for 5 weeks! Mexico, here I come!

JULY 17 – THE FIRST DAY!
We made it all the way to Ogden, Utah today. We drove through 5 states, just like that, and now we're here. We got a nice motel with a pool. Eight of us girls are sharing a room; we have 4 double beds. This morning at 5:30, we all met at the college parking lot and loaded our stuff into a big van with lots of windows. Ten people rode in the van, four people rode a blue Chevy, and two women and four little boys rode in a white station wagon. We left at 6:05 A.M., right on schedule, and I very quickly made about 7 friends. We had lunch in Boise, Idaho, and made a few other quick stops to get gas. I slept and wrote letters most of the ride. I also talked quite a lot.

When we first checked into the motel rooms, the girls went to eat right away, but the guys and I went for a swim first. (We are 13 women, 4 men and 4 little boys.) Then Bart took me to dinner. Why me? He has singled me out and has been spending lots of time with me, while all the other girls are free to do girl-things together, whatever they are, I have *never done them. (Seems like I'm always with a guy.) After we ate, Bart took me for a walk. I'm having a good time so far. Really good!*

Could this be a real diary? Was it true? Who had written it, Crystal wondered. She heard the kids come into the house and she quickly returned the diary to its hiding place. She noiselessly eased down the steps into the library and sat in a chair facing the window, acting as if she had been sitting there the whole time they were outside.

"Crystal, come and ride bikes around the property with us," Taylor said, coming into the library. "The path is so neat, and it's paved the whole way. You can see everything from the path, the whole property."

Crystal did not respond.

"Taylor, come on," Crystal heard one of the twins yell from the other room, "we can make it around one more time before it gets dark, if we hurry."

"Come on, don't be like that," Taylor said to Crystal. "Oh, that's right, you have to mourn forever. Well, I'm finished mourning. You're going to have to be sad all by yourself." Taylor left her sitting there.

Crystal didn't move until she saw them ride away from the house, then she went back up the steps to get the diary again. Just as she was about to resume reading, she heard voices from the hallway outside the library. From where she was, she couldn't be seen from downstairs, and that was the way she wanted it. She didn't want anyone to know she was up there.

"Let's go in the library, Dad," she heard a man say.

"Son, you are looking healthy, but mighty thin," Pastor Young said, as they entered the library.

"Dad, it's about Randall. I don't want Rachel to know."

"What is it, Vance? Is he hurt? Is he in some kind of trouble?"

"He's... well... missing."

"Missing? What do you mean?"

"He's been kidnapped. We were both stationed in Central America – see this map? – right down here, and he was kidnapped by revolutionaries. He is being held hostage, but our government refuses to acknowledge it. They say he ran away, that he is a deserter, but I was there. I overheard the officers talking about the ransom, and they said he's not worth it, because of some secret mission. If they admit that he's being held hostage, it could compromise the entire operation.

"The reason they chose Randall for this mission, I guess, is because we're orphans. You and Mom aren't our legal relatives, so they figured he had nothing to lose. No one would miss him or cause a problem if he got into trouble. One other guy, Morton, another guy without any family, was sent with Randall, and Morton escaped to tell me what happened and exactly where they are holding him. Randall is being held right here, in this jungle, near this ancient city, just down this river. Then the next say, Morton disappeared – I think our guys took him out so he wouldn't blow their cover. But I know where Randall is – I just can't go back and help him. Dad, they are shipping me to the Middle East."

"What? When?"

"When I started asking questions about Randall, they immediately prepared my transfer. They gave me no choice in the matter. I begged the officer who was arranging my flights to let me have a stopover in Portland – so he gave me just 12 hours. I have to catch my flight in the morning back to the base, and I'll fly out from there."

"Randall will be alright," Pastor Young assured him. "Son, let's pray for your brother right now," Pastor Young said. "Father, in the name of Your Son, Jesus, we are asking right now for Your hedge of protection around Randall. We are asking for Your mercies to encompass him and comfort him. We pray that You give him favor with his captors, that You touch him and strengthen him and encourage him by Your mighty power and Your Word. Lord, You have provided him with a young family, and we ask that You allow him to return safely to his family. Touch him, right now, in Jesus' name we pray, amen."

"Dad, we have to do something. Every day they hold Randall, the slimmer his chances of surviving. We don't have much time."

"God is already doing something."

"Dad--"

"Don't worry. Don't you know it's a sin to worry?"

"Yes, sir."

"Do you trust God to take care of everything?"

"Yes, sir."

"It's already done. Now you have to get ready for your next mission."

"What are you going to tell Rachel?"

"I don't know yet, but God has never steered me wrong before," Pastor Young said. "He'll give me the right words to say."

"Dad, remember that time God told you to go over to the Morehouse farm – you had never been there before – and He told you to go? And right when you got there, you saved me from drowning in their pond?"

"I remember like it was yesterday. I can't forget any of the great things God has done for me, for us, for all of us. He's been too good to forget."

"Every time we got in trouble, you were always there."

"God always sent me."

"I'm glad you always obeyed Him."

"It's the only way," Pastor Young agreed. "Now let's go spend a few minutes with your mother and sister-in-law before you have to go."

They left the library and Crystal tried to make sense of what she had just heard. Randall had been kidnapped in another country and Vance was being sent to another part of the world, yet Pastor Young didn't seem at all upset by the news. They had no idea she had been up there, listening. Well, she had no problem keeping a secret, since she wasn't planning to talk to anybody anyway. Now she couldn't even talk to that traitor, Taylor, which was just as well. She didn't want to share any secrets with her anyway.

Crystal wasn't in the mood for reading any more now. She slipped the diary back into its hiding place and quietly went downstairs and into her room. She sat on the bed and then leaned back onto the pillow. She would have fallen asleep if the door hadn't burst open with Kenny, Keith and Taylor laughing and tumbling into the room.

"Hey, do you want some home-made ice cream?" one of the twins asked her. She didn't answer.

"You can just nod for yes or shake your head for no," he suggested. Taylor and the other twin giggled.

"It's really good," he said. "Grandma always makes it when we come over."

"If Crystal wants some, she can come and get it," Taylor said, leading the boys out of the room.

Crystal didn't want any ice cream. She didn't want anything but to fade into nothingness, where she wouldn't have to listen to laughter and problems and life going on all around her. She sat still for quite a long time, but sleep wouldn't come. She wasn't worrying about anything; she wasn't even thinking about anything. She was just waiting for sleep, but it would not overtake her.

"Crystal?" Sister Young's voice asked, as the light flickered and then lit up the room. "Are you sure you don't want some ice cream?"

As usual, she answered with silence.

"Well, why don't you come on out here with us? We're all going up to look at the stars from the top of the library tower."

Crystal stood and followed Sister Young down the hall to the library, and up the stairs to the top deck, where the open door revealed millions of stars in the sky. The whole group stood silent, looking at the stars and the blackness of the night. Only a few distant lights could be seen, including the outline of the cross on the chapel building. Crystal hadn't known there were so many stars. When Daddy used to take her and Taylor out to the lake in Tennessee and they looked up at the stars, there seemed to be only a small fraction of the number she could see now. Here, they looked so close, as if they were just beyond reach, like random sparkles in a huge, black blanket.

Crystal noticed another difference here: where were all the bugs? They were not engulfed by zillions of bugs as they always had been at this time of the year back home; they were not being eaten alive by mosquitoes. She could hear a lot of frogs croaking, and a gentle breeze was causing a distant swishing of the trees in the surrounding forests. The moon lit the landscape with a bluish tint, and as her eyes adjusted to the dark, Crystal began to recognize the buildings, the orchard, and the different areas of the property. She thought she saw a movement down near the pond. She stared but couldn't see anything.

"Look at the deer," Pastor Young said quietly. As Crystal looked, the outline of three deer seemed to be drawn on the darkened landscape. They stood frozen for a moment, then they glided to the pond to drink.

"Where's the Big Dipper?" a twin whispered.

"Right up there," Vance pointed. In the moonlight, Crystal could see that Vance was tall and very handsome, a little older than the picture of him and Randall in the dining room, and now with much shorter hair. Keith and Kenny looked just like miniature versions of their uncle.

"Oh, yeah! Hey, it was right there when we were here last summer."

"Where's the Little Dipper?" the other twin asked.

"Follow those two stars – see the North Star there? Okay, it's right up there."

"I see it! For the first time in my life, I see the Little Dipper!" the twin said excitedly.

"Where?" the other twin asked.

"Right up there," his brother pointed.

"Oh, yeah! I see it! Cool!"

"Watch what you're doing, Spilly McSpillerson! You just dumped your water on me."

"Sorry, Edgy McEdgerson."

"You should be."

"You should be!"

"Boys, didn't your mother talk to you about this earlier?" Pastor Young asked.

"We are outside, we can use our outside voices."

"Boys! Do not talk back to your grandfather," Rachel said.

"Yes, ma'am," they said together. "Sorry, Granddad."

The entire group stood for several minutes without talking, just enjoying the view on this warm summer night. Crystal wondered if God was closer to them up here, just behind that blanket with the stars; then she realized that He was still as far away from her as He could possibly be. He had left her alone, and He didn't care about her at all. If God had really cared for her, He wouldn't have taken her father away from her.

CHAPTER 7

Vance left later that night just before everyone went to bed. Crystal slept as late the next morning as she possibly could; she had not been awakened by Taylor when she got dressed to go and play with the twins. She avoided the other kids all day. Later, in the evening, Crystal sneaked upstairs to read more of the diary. No one seemed to notice where she was going and what she was doing. She almost felt as if she had disappeared again, like she had at school when she had become invisible.

Back home, after the other kids had had their fill of teasing her, and she refused to react to them, she became invisible. Nobody talked to her, nobody played with her, nobody ate lunch with her. Nobody could see her any more. She was glad, because as long as they didn't see her, they didn't see that she was different, and they didn't bother her. She didn't need to be seen at school. She didn't need to have friends at school, because her daddy gave her all the love she needed. He had more love than anyone, for his daughters. He had reassured her when she was in the first grade and the kids first started being mean to her, that no matter who didn't like her, or how many kids made fun of her dark skin, he loved her enough to fill any wound made by their hateful remarks. After he told her that, their words bounced off of her like arrows hitting a shield. Their hostility could not penetrate her mind or her heart. Soon they no longer saw her, they no longer bothered her. Her invisibility became her safe place, the refuge where she stayed while she was at school. She was able to go anywhere in the building or on the school grounds and she couldn't be seen. She didn't need to hide because nobody could see her.

She felt the same way now. Pastor Young and Sister Young continued to talk to her, as if they expected an answer from her at any time, but she knew they had something much more important on their minds now. They didn't really see her. She opened to the next entry in the diary.

FRIDAY, JULY 18

This morning we were awakened at 6:30 by Mr. Hanson's 6 phone calls. We ate breakfast and left Ogden by 8:00 a.m.

Bart and I spent about 3 hours naming Beatle songs. We stopped for lunch in Shiprock, Utah. Then Jane drove for awhile, and Bart and I practiced Spanish for a long time. He's pretty good, and not as shy about using it as I am. We hit a construction area, which slowed us down, then we had to stop for cattle crossing (cows actually walking across the road!) Jane took us through Colorado and Bart started driving in New Mexico. We were behind a huge oil truck when it hit a big patch of water in the road. With all our windows down, we got drenched -- but we were so hot, it felt good!

I am learning how to sleep in any position: sitting up, with head on knees while sitting, with head in lap while sitting. I could probably even sleep standing up! I slept until we reached Gallup, New Mexico, where we're staying tonight. Almost everyone went to dinner right away, but I wasn't hungry. Bart was depressed. (Why?) (I didn't know guys got depressed.) I tried to cheer him up. I guess I did a good job, because in about an hour he felt better and we went to eat dinner. I wanted to call my grandmother in Santa Fe, but the switchboard at our motel was already off for the night. I'll call her tomorrow morning.

Now that I'm a few pages into this, I want to describe some of the people on the trip with me. I have already mentioned Bart. He won't say how old he is... 19 or 20? He always talks in riddles, or lines from songs. He's really clever and witty; quick. And he's cuuuute! He is about 6 feet or taller, has broad shoulders, deep, brown eyes, a nice smile, brown, wavy hair. I have been spending most of my time (so far) on this trip with him. He loves music, but isn't a very good singer. He seems like a normal, decent guy.

The other male student is Diego. He is tall, (though not as tall as Bart,) handsome, with black hair, dark brown eyes, dark skin and a nice smile that reveals a mouth full of straight, white teeth. He has a real sense of humor, and

61

although he's usually quiet, when he talks, he says just the right thing to make us laugh. He is Mexican- American and speaks Spanish very well. He is 19 and already in junior college.

Lisa is from Spokane, the one I noticed at the meeting. She is also 17. She and I are the youngest in the group. (Actually, she is the youngest; I am 5 days older than she is.) She has fine, blond, wavy hair to her shoulders and clear blue eyes. Her skin is very fair. She has been riding in the front passenger seat of the van the whole time, away from the rest of us and our conversations. She seems really shy and withdrawn, maybe nervous about something, maybe homesick already? But I like her. There's something special about her. We could become good friends, if we get to spend time together and know each other. I hope we get that chance!

Then there's Diana. She is 19. She has to get up two hours before everyone else does, because that's how long it takes to put on her make-up. She curls each hair with a hot comb, and her hair is a bleached orange-blond color, totally unnatural. She wears at least 3 layers of make-up on her face, and four kinds around her eyes, and two colors of lipstick! Also, she has a loud, screechy, irritating voice, and she's always smacking her gum. Early this morning I got up to go to the bathroom when Diana was starting to put on her make-up. I saw her with her natural face, and she looked like a completely different person! She didn't look bad without make-up. I thought she looked better, but she is addicted to make-up! She can't let anyone see her without it, and I was just lucky to have caught her off guard. (Lucky me!)

Diana's friend, Jane, is also 19. They both go to college with Diego. Jane looks natural and only wears a little mascara. She's very attractive. She is quiet and smiling most of the time, a cute, crooked little smile, and she laughs at whatever Diana says. I've seen how Diego looks at her. He likes her. I think she likes him, too, but when she's with Diana, which is most of the time, they both ignore Diego. Jane would rather go with Diana anywhere than do something with Diego.

Then there are Sharon, a large woman; Lou, a high school

PE teacher; Theresa, Lou's friend; Ricardo, our Spanish teacher; his wife, Nancy, and their four boys (ages 2, 4, 6, and 8); Gregg, our history teacher (who doesn't know any Spanish); Anita, a small, rich widow, Alice, who smiles all the time and chatters a lot and knows Spanish well; Christi, who is 19, and Linda, who is very nice, quiet, with long, blond hair.

I'm 17, have long, medium brown, curly hair and brown eyes. I smile a lot. I know how to read and write in Spanish, but am shy about speaking it. I like math and art, and I like to try new things. I'm learning photography, and I love to take pictures! I also love to write. I write poems, journals, stories, articles, books, and letters. I hope to have at least 5 books published while I'm still in my teens. I have 2 books finished already, one I wrote when I was 10 and the other when I was 13, and several more in progress.

This is the summer before my senior year in high school. I'm ready for anything. I don't have any hang-ups; I'm not afraid of anything! I'm just a normal 17-year-old girl on a big adventure. And I like guys.

Out of all these girls, why did Bart pick me? He's so cute, why me? Are we alike? We do both like music, jokes and puns, and witty answers -- but I'm not ready for any type of relationship at all now. (That's why I broke up with Mike.) Bart and I are just friends. It's nice to have a friend.

Crystal came back to the present when she heard voices in the library.

"She doesn't need to know right now how serious it is," Pastor Young was saying.

"Have you told her anything at all about where Randall is?" Sister Young asked.

"No. I think we both need to tell her together, but without all the details."

"Yeah, that's a good idea. She would be so worried, she wouldn't be able to take care of her boys. With their father gone, they don't need their mother to be all messed up. Let's let her sleep now, and tell her in the morning."

"Tomorrow I'm going to make some phone calls and see if I can get some answers," Pastor Young said. "They can't send someone into a dangerous situation just because he doesn't have a family, and then just act like he never existed."

"He *does* have a family. We are his family."

"I know. He's our son. But they don't have us in his records as his legal family. We are listed as his emergency contacts. According to the military, Randall has no family at all, except Vance, and they consider him to be equally as expendable. They don't realize that the bond of love is stronger than being legally related."

"Much prayer is needed," Sister Young said softly.

"That's all we can do now," Pastor Young agreed. They said a prayer for Randall, Vance and Rachel, and for God to give them direction in this matter. Then they left the library. Crystal stayed in her hiding place for a long time, not wanting anyone to discover where she had been spending her time, and especially not wanting them to know that she had been listening to their private conversations. She would never say a word about what she had heard; nor would she say a word about anything at all, to anyone, not even to Taylor.

When Crystal felt it was safe for her to escape without being seen, she slipped down the steps and across the hall into her room. She did not wait for Taylor; she fell asleep almost immediately.

Crystal sat up straight in bed. The room was completely dark. She had had the dream again, only this time Daddy had started to tell her something. As she arrived by his side, he asked her, "Honey, why didn't you –" and then he closed his eyes: she opened hers, to this room. What had he wanted her to do? What didn't she do for him? What could she have done to alter the outcome of that horrendous evening?

Everything seemed so plain to her, at this quiet time in the middle of the night. She had neglected Daddy in some way. She had disappointed him. She had not done something he had expected her to do. If she had just done that one thing, whatever it might have been, Daddy would still be alive today.

Crystal looked over to where Taylor was sleeping. The room was too dark to see her; she heard her rhythmic breathing. Taylor didn't have the dream anymore. She was letting Daddy go. Maybe she was too young to remember things, to remember how Daddy was their whole world. Maybe she didn't care about their past and about her own sister. Maybe she was like everyone else, just trying to fit into their world, their silly jokes, their senseless sporting events, their constant competition.

Crystal didn't feel disappointed that her sister was deserting her. Taylor was choosing her own path, apart from Crystal, and her decision did not impact Crystal at all in any way. Nothing could make Crystal mad, nothing could make her happy. Nothing could make her feel anything at all, ever.

CHAPTER 8

The next morning, Crystal was awakened early when Sister Young came into the room.

"Girls, let's get up and get ready for church," she said cheerfully. "If you get up now, you have time to take a shower and eat some breakfast."

Crystal heard Taylor moving around in her bed.

"We always go to church on Sunday morning," Sister Young said. "The whole family goes together. We don't leave anyone at home when we go to church."

Crystal didn't want to argue with Sister Young that she was not a part of the family, so she silently got out of bed and began to get ready to go to church. She didn't have a dress or any fancy shoes to wear, so she chose one of her few outfits. She didn't feel the need to dress up to go to God's house, because He didn't care if she went there or not; He didn't care about her at all.

As they gathered around the breakfast table, Crystal looked at Rachel to see if she looked any different. Had they told her about Randall yet? She was not showing any sign that she knew. Maybe she was good at hiding her feelings. The twins poked at each other, quietly, though, smiling and laughing and trying to entertain Taylor. Right now they could be proud of their father, a soldier in the army. They didn't realize that their whole world could come crashing down on them in one second, the second that they heard the bad news that he was being held hostage, or that he had been killed. They had no idea that their hopes and dreams could be crushed in the instant that they learned that their father would never be coming home to them again.

Crystal pushed her food around her plate, not listening to the table conversation, until Pastor Young announced that it was time for them to go. Rachel cleared the table while Sister Young wiped Kenny's face and brushed Keith's hair. Pastor Young picked up his Bible and opened the front door. The group filed out of the house and walked down the path to the chapel.

When they arrived, an old farmer was already there, leaning against the front door. His skin was the same color as Crystal's, only his was a tan. He was dressed in pinstriped overalls and was wearing a big straw hat.

"Morning, Pastor Young," he said.

"Good morning, Papa Brown," Pastor Young said enthusiastically. "Where is Mother Brown this morning?"

"She's already inside. We walked this morning and she needed to get off her feet."

"Good for you! How was the walk?"

"Wonderful, wonderful. We couldn't ask for a nicer day."

"God is good," Pastor Young said.

"All the time," Papa Brown replied.

"Look who we brought with us," Pastor Young said, as Rachel and her boys came around the corner and down the path.

"Well, bless my soul," Papa Brown said, "if it isn't my lovely little Rachel and your two boys – my, my, my, they have grown since last summer!"

"And these are our two girls, Crystal and Taylor, who have come to stay with us," Sister Young said. "Girls, this is Papa Brown, one of the elders of our church."

"So glad to meet you," Papa Brown said, tipping his hat. "So you finally got the daughters you've been praying for, Sister Young," he said with a wide smile.

"God answers prayer," she replied with a smile.

The whole group entered the church and immediately Crystal sensed a completely different type of atmosphere: stillness. They held hands in the foyer and said a prayer, then they went into the sanctuary. Pastor Young went up to the pulpit while the rest of them selected seats. Even the boys were reverent in this place. A few more people came inside and Sister Young gave each person a hug as Pastor Young stood up to begin the worship services. Crystal glanced around and saw about 45 people wearing various types of clothing had gathered and were all seated near the pulpit.

"Good morning," Pastor Young said.

"Good morning," the congregation replied.

"How many know that God has been good?" Pastor Young asked.

"All the time!" everybody shouted.

"Did He wake you up this morning, in your right mind? Did He give you the activities of your limbs? Did He make it possible for you to be here today, to give Him the glory?

"Somebody might say, 'my alarm clock woke me up this morning,' or 'my mother woke me up this morning,' but do you realize that if God hadn't touched you, you wouldn't have been able to get up? Somebody got up this morning and found that a loved one slipped away during the night, that God had taken him or her home. The alarm clock could be ringing all morning, and that person couldn't get up, no matter how much the family members shouted or shook him.

"Only God can wake us up and give us life and health and strength, and even a beautiful day like today! The weather man might try to tell us what the weather will be, and he's usually wrong, because God does whatever He wants to do! Today, He chose to give us a beautiful, sunny day, and, as His Word says, 'This is the day that the Lord has made,' and I will what? Rejoice! And be glad in it! Are you glad today? I'm glad! I'm so glad!

"Let us have an opening prayer," Pastor Young said. "Father in heaven, we thank You today for this beautiful day that You have made. We thank You for bringing us together one more time, to worship You and to praise You. We love You today, and we ask that You have Your way in the service. Fill us with Your Spirit today! We love You, Lord! We thank You, Lord! In Jesus' mighty name we pray, Amen."

Members of the congregation were shouting "Amen!" "Yeah!" and "That's right!" as Pastor Young was praying, getting louder and louder as the excitement was growing. Crystal could tell this was not going to be like the church services she had attended in Tennessee. Back home, when they had gone with Tammy to church, the pews were crowded and everyone sat quietly while the seven or eight people in the pulpit went through their rituals. Every time they had gone to church, it was exactly the same: the same people read the same prayers, the same scripture verses and they sang the same three songs. The service started at exactly 8:00 and they were finished at exactly 9:00 on Sunday morning. They didn't have to go to church every week, only when Tammy needed something from God.

"Deacon Eagle, will you read find an opening scripture for us this morning?"

"I've got one ready," a well-built, dark-haired young man said. "Psalm 8."

"Let's all turn to Psalm 8 in our Bibles," Pastor Young said, as people opened their Bibles and turned pages. Crystal didn't reach for a Bible from the back of the pew in front of her. She just sat still, not reacting.

"Let us stand for the reading of the Word," Pastor Young instructed. "If you are able to stand on your feet, let's do this to honor God's Word." Crystal stood beside Taylor, who had opened a Bible to the correct page.

Deacon Eagle read the scripture, but Crystal wasn't listening. She wondered how long the service would last. She was pretty sure it would be longer than one hour; not that it mattered. She didn't have anywhere else to go or anything else to do.

"You may be seated," Pastor Young said, when Deacon Eagle had finished reading. "Who has a testimony this morning? We should all have something to say about how good the LORD has been. Hasn't He been good?"

"Amen! Yes, He has!" people shouted in response. An older man stood to his feet.

"Go ahead, Farmer Scott," Pastor Young said.

"Pastor, I want to thank the Lord for bringing back my Nadine," he began, then paused while the congregation cheered and shouted and thanked God. He turned to look at an old woman who was seated beside him. "I don't want to take her testimony, but God healed her of cancer."

"Amen! Hallelujah!" the church members shouted.

69

"The doctors said she would be dead by today, but here she is," Farmer Scott continued. "I want to thank everyone for your prayers. When we came by here last week, on our way to the hospital, we all prayed and believed God for a miracle. He answered our prayers! Thank You, Jesus!"

"Glory to God! Amen!"

"We went up to the hospital and they said they weren't sure if they could do surgery, because they said the lump was in her brain, and if they did the surgery, she might not live, or she might be a vegetable. They showed us the X-ray and we could see this dark spot, right back here. They said it was growing fast, and if they didn't remove it, she would die in just a few days. I told them that they might not be able to do anything for her, but that my God could heal her. Pastor, they looked at me like I was crazy, but I know what God can do. Well, they kept her for a day, then they decided to do another X-ray from another angle. Do you know, they couldn't find the lump? It was gone! God had healed her already!"

"Praise God! Hallelujah!"

"The doctors couldn't believe it, so they did a bunch more tests. They couldn't find a spot at all! I told them that my God is more powerful than any cancer, and that He has more healing in the hem of His garment than all the drugstores in the land! Stand up, Honey, so everyone can see what God has done."

Nadine stood up and looked around at everyone, smiling.

"He is good," she said.

"All the time!" everybody shouted, applauding.

"I'll never forget the look on their faces when they saw the second X-ray," she said, speaking slowly. "Then they did one of those brain scan things because they were sure they somehow missed the lump. But they couldn't find anything because God healed me!" she said. She began jumping up and down, and tears streamed down her face.

"Glory to God! Hallelujah! Praise Him! Praise Him!"

The church members were shouting so loudly, Crystal thought they might have been at a football game, cheering on their team. How could they get so excited about God? Weren't they supposed to be quiet, and silently beg God for what they wanted?

A young man appeared at they piano and began to play a song Crystal had never heard before, and everyone started singing 'I'm so glad Jesus lifted me.' People were playing tambourines and jumping up and down and singing loudly. When the song ended, they all started shouting 'Hallelujah!'

"Let's give the Lord a hand praise," Pastor Young said, clapping his hands. Everybody else joined him, and the clapping sounded like a roaring.

"Isn't God good?" Pastor Young said. "I want to thank Him for my family. Don't they look nice this morning?" he asked, and was answered by a hundred amens. Crystal felt people were looking at her, since she was sitting at the end of the pew by Taylor, who was next to the twins and Rachel and Sister Young. "Our daughter-in-law is here today with two of our grandchildren, and we have two new daughters with us today. Girls, why don't you stand up so everyone can see you?"

Taylor immediately obeyed and Crystal reluctantly stood also.

"This is Crystal, the older one, and her sister, Taylor, and they have come to live with us. We are so blessed by them being here, and I'm sure you all will love them too. Boys, stand up too, so everyone can see how much you've grown. We want to continue to pray for their father, our son, Randall, and for their Uncle Vance, who are both still in the military, serving our country. They are dealing with some things and they need a miracle. I don't need to go into the details, but God knows all about them, and He is able to do all things but fail. Isn't He able?"

Pastor Young was answered by cheers and shouts of "Amen!"

"Do we have another testimony?" A heavy woman in too-tight evening clothes jumped to her feet. "Sister Noreen, go right ahead."

"Well, I just want to thank the Lord for not putting me out of my house like my landlord said he would, but God worked a miracle and provided me with a way to stay there, and I want to thank Him for putting food on my table, so I am not starving, like I could be if the devil had his way, and even though I got fired from my job last week, the one I just started, God blessed me to find another job the same day and my boss of my old job told me I would have to work on Sundays and I told him there was no way I was going to work on the Lord's day, but that I had to give the whole day to the Lord, so my boss told me I better find a job somewhere else, and I told him I would, so God just shut one door and opened another one on the same day," she said, all in one breath. Her voice was high and whiney as she continued, "so I went to the business next door to where I was working and they are closed on Sundays so I wouldn't have to work on Sundays and I asked them if they had an opening and the secretary sent me to the back room with the boss and I told him he needed me and I would do anything to work for him because I was desperate for a job and he looked at me and said he thought he could use me and the next thing I knew, he was hiring me and I was starting to work as his assistant, and that was God opening that door for me! Nobody but God could do that, nobody but God would do that kind of thing for me, or for anyone, and I know that God is so good and He will never let us down and He will never leave us alone, but He is always with us, no matter what we do or how bad we mess up or who hates us or who is trying to put us down or how the devil wants to hurt us and hold us back. I just want to say that God is blessing me each and every day, in every way and He is going to give me my son back, I believe that, and I am going to go back to school, God is going to open that door for me too, I made some phone calls this week and--"

"Don't try to tell it all, Sister," Pastor Young said.

"I won't try to tell it all," she repeated, "or we would be here all afternoon and all night and all day tomorrow and all week until next week, and then I would lose my new job if

I didn't show up, but I have a lot to say about God and how good He is and how good He has been and everything, He is everything I need, my Provider and my Caretaker and my Teacher and my Counselor and my Doctor and my Lawyer and a Mother to the motherless and a Father to the fatherless and a Husband to the husbandless; He is my Husband, and I know He can do everything and He has been so good to me, and He is everything to me, and I just want to sing a song!" she shouted, stepping up to the pulpit and reaching for the microphone.

"Can you save the song for later?" Pastor Young asked. "We want to give everyone a chance to testify."

"Oh, all right," Sister Noreen whined as she returned to her seat.

"Brother Erickson, go right ahead," Pastor Young said to a tall, thin, blonde young man who was standing.

"I just want to thank the Lord," he said slowly and deliberately, looking at a small boy seated beside him, "for taking care of me and my son, Eric Junior, since the Lord took his mama home last year. The Lord sent workers to help me with my crop, so I can be at home more and take care of Eric. God has healed our hurt and we just want to thank Him. I couldn't make it without the Lord."

"Did you all hear what Brother Erickson just said?" Pastor Young asked. "Only with the LORD can we make it. We can't do it ourselves. God will send His Comforter to be with us, and to fill that space, when we are hurting."

Crystal did not agree. She hadn't felt any comfort from God at all. She didn't see or feel anything that God was doing in her life. These people didn't know what they were saying. They didn't know what she needed. Her situation was much worse than anyone else's situation. God wouldn't want to do anything for her. If He did, He would have done it already. He would not have let her dad die. He had already let the worst thing in the world happen to her.

Several more people stood up and told about what God was doing in their lives, with more shouting and clapping from the congregation. Everybody sang another song that Crystal hadn't heard before, about having victory in the name of Jesus. Then Pastor Young said a very long prayer for all the people in hospitals and in nursing homes, and for the people in the military, and for the families of everyone who was in the church today, and for everyone who was worshipping in all churches this morning. He kept telling God how much they all loved Him and kept thanking Him for being so good. Crystal had never heard a prayer like this one.

When Pastor Young finished praying, everybody started singing another song about Jesus that Crystal didn't know, something about knowing that He lives because He lives in their hearts. Pastor Young announced that it was time for giving, and two people went up to the front and set several baskets on a small table. Crystal and Taylor didn't have any money. Pastor Young prayed a short prayer, saying that they should always thank God in advance for what He was going to do, then he asked everybody to come forth, even if they didn't have anything, and at least touch the baskets. Crystal followed the people in her row around and was surprised when she glanced in the baskets to see how much had been given by this relatively small crowd. One of the men standing said a prayer of thanks for the gifts and the givers, and for those who wanted to give but had nothing to give.

"Let us all stand to our feet for a couple of verses of 'Amazing Grace,'" Pastor Young said. Everybody stood up and sang the song from memory. Crystal did not sing with them. She didn't like to sing. She remembered that Daddy had said that he always had music playing in his head, but she didn't. Her head was silent.

Crystal let her mind wander while Pastor Young talked about Jesus. He read something from the Bible, but Crystal wasn't paying attention. She guessed that as long as they lived with the Youngs, she would have to come to church every Sunday; but she didn't have to participate. She didn't have to participate in life.

After the sermon, Pastor Young stepped down from the

pulpit and stood in front of the pews. One man set a chair beside Pastor Young.

"Maybe you don't know Jesus Christ as your Lord and Savior," Pastor Young said. "Maybe you feel the Lord is speaking to you right now. If that is you, you can come now." Taylor looked at Crystal, who stared straight ahead without reacting. Pastor Young paused for a moment, extending his hand. Nobody moved.

"If you are out of a church home, maybe you feel God is leading you to be a part of this church family. You can come now," Pastor Young said, his hand still extended. "I always say, a Christian out of a church home is like a fish out of water. And how long will he live? He will not live very long. It's the same with the Christian; not that he necessarily will die physically, which is possible, but he will die spiritually, if he is not being spiritually fed. If you are out of a church home, you can come now.

"Maybe you need special prayer. Maybe you have been praying and you feel that your prayers are not getting any higher than the ceiling. Maybe you have an appointment this week – how many have an appointment this week?" Several people raised their hands. "I see a few hands being raised. Maybe you have a situation that only God can solve. I know I do." Pastor Young raised his hands. "I've got both hands raised. Let us pray for all those needs, that God will give us favor in every situation.

"Father God, in the name of Jesus, we pray for the needs of everyone here. You know each need, and only You can supply those needs. You told us to ask, and we would receive, and Father, we are asking You today. You told us to seek and we would find. We are seeking You today, Father, and we are knocking, expecting the door to be opened for us. Lord, every need is in Your hands, our very lives are in Your hands, and we thank You in advance for what You are going to do this week. In Jesus' name we pray, and let the church say, Amen."

"Amen," the congregation repeated.

"Repeat after me: Let the words of my mouth..." Pastor Young said.

"Let the words of my mouth…" they repeated.

"…and the meditation of my heart…"

"…and the meditation of my heart…"

"…be acceptable in Thy sight…"

"…be acceptable in Thy sight…"

"…oh, Lord, my Strength and my Redeemer."

"…oh, Lord, my Strength and my Redeemer."

"In Jesus' name, amen, amen and amen," Pastor Young said. "Give somebody a hug and tell them that you love them!"

People began moving around, hugging and talking and touching each other. Crystal cringed when an old lady came up to her and gave her a gentle hug.

"I am your nearest neighbor, Marge," she said with a soft voice. "We live – my husband, Henry, right over there, and I – just across the road on that side. If you need anything, you just come right across the road and see us. We are home all the time, well, except on Sundays, of course, when we are here. So where are you from?"

Crystal didn't answer.

"Oh, you don't have to be shy with me," she said kindly, trying to look into Crystal's eyes. Crystal turned her eyes to the floor.

"She can't talk!" one of the twins shouted.

"Yeah, she can't talk," the other twin repeated.

"Don't waste your time," the first twin said.

"Yeah, don't waste your time," the other one repeated.

"You boys certainly have grown," Marge said. "However, you have not grown up enough that you can tell a grownup what to do."

"Yes, ma'am."

"Sorry, ma'am."

"Let's go talk to Ronnie!" They began to run toward the door.

"Boys! You know better than to run in the sanctuary!" Rachel scolded them. They slowed to a quick walk and went out the door.

"You don't have to talk to me," Marge said. "If you would like to just come over and sit with me, or make cookies with me, or ride one of our horses, feel free. Our door is always open to our neighbors. Bring your sister with you, if you like." She paused, then she said, "It is very nice meeting you. I know you will like it here. I look forward to seeing you again soon."

Crystal waited until Marge walked away, then she followed Taylor out the door, while people were still hugging and talking. The twins were outside with a dark-haired boy who was about Crystal's age.

"Taylor! Come and meet Ronnie!" one twin shouted.

"Ronnie, this is Taylor. She's kind of like our cousin."

"Or your aunt," Taylor said.

"Yeah, like our aunt. Our cousin-aunt."

"Our aunt-cousin."

"Nice to meet you," Taylor said politely.

"Likewise. Is that your sister?" Ronnie asked her.

"Yeah, but she can't talk," one of the twins said.

"Yeah, she can't talk."

"Is 'Ronnie' your nick name? Or your real name?" Taylor asked.

"It's my nick name," he said.

"So what's your real name?" Taylor asked. "Ronald?"

"Ronald McDonald!" the twins shouted together. "Ronald McDonald!"

"No! It's not Ronald!" Ronnie insisted.

"Then what is it?" Taylor asked.

"Ronald McDonald!"

"It's not Ronald!"

"Maybe it's Veronica. Mom has a friend named Veronica and everyone calls her Ronnie."

"Veronica? That's a girl's name," Taylor said.

"It's NOT Veronica!" Ronnie insisted.

"Then what is it?"

"It's Hieronymous, okay?"

"Hieronymous? Really?"

"Hieronymous?" Taylor asked. "Why'd your mom name you that?"

"I have no idea," Ronnie said, shaking his head. The twins stood without speaking for a moment. "Well, let's go to the pond and catch some frogs," Ronnie suggested.

"Yeah, let's go!" one twin shouted.

"Mom! We're going to the pond!" the other twin yelled.

"Don't fall in," Rachel replied.

"We won't!" they shouted, as they began running down the trail to the pond.

Taylor waited by Crystal for a minute, then she too ran down the trail, following the boys toward the pond. Crystal stood by the church building and waited for Sister Young to come outside. She stayed out of sight so none of the other people would ask her any questions. After Sister Young finished hugging everybody who was outside, Crystal followed her and Rachel up the hill. She could hear the kids shouting at the pond as she made her way through the woods to the house. When they arrived at the house, she went into her room and sat on the bed for a few minutes, then she sneaked to the library and tiptoed up the steps. She pulled the diary from its hiding place, sunk down into one of the large pillows, and began to read the next entry.

SUNDAY, JULY 20

Mexico! This is great! The first thing I noticed when we came into Chihuahua was the temperature displayed on the bank. It was only 28 degrees, but so hot! Then I remembered Mexico uses the Metric system. Ah, yes. I was all excited, and I mentioned it to the others, and they all just said, "Oh." Oh, well. I thought it was great. It was the first cultural difference I noticed when we got here!

I'm so thankful, my prayer was answered: Lisa and I get to share a room in a home with some really nice people. Our "father," Miguel, and our "mother," Cande, are in their early 20's. They have a baby girl, Lili, who is only 3 months old. Miguel has straight, black hair and a mustache. Cande is just a couple years older than we are, and she is very beautiful, with long, black hair. El señor tries to speak English, but he can't speak it very well. My Spanish isn't too great, either. I only spoke to them for a few minutes when I first got here. I like it here, I'm not nervous. I feel relaxed and just fine, but not relaxed enough to go around speaking Spanish out loud!

We have a radio in our room and we have already discovered a couple of stations where the music is basically the same as we listen to in the states, with some Mexican songs mixed in.

I really love this trip. I don't see how anyone can get "down," like Bart did. I cheered him up, but he's down again. He should be happy just because of this fun trip, all these new and outrageous people... and we're in MEXICO!!! (Yeah, I talk to Bart a lot. Is that bad? We speak a lot of Spanish to each other. That is good.)

This is wonderful. Fantastic. What more can I say? Besides good night, buenas noches!

MONDAY MORNING, JULY 21

Talk about strange. The family has a baby and a kitten. The kitten was crying all night, outside our window, keeping us awake. Our 'mother' doesn't know English, and it is difficult to communicate with her. This morning, I hit my head on a model airplane hanging in the room, then kicked the leg of the bed and hurt my toe. I almost fell over in a chair, then I smashed my hand in the closet door. Que malo suerte!

We're getting ready to go to school! Adios para ahora.

MONDAY AFTERNOON, STILL JULY 21

I am sitting on the bed with the kitten in my lap.

I love Chihuahua! It is a very beautiful city! We walked to school today, our first day. We decided which classes were which, then Bart, Diego and I went to the bank to cash traveler's checks, and I felt so rich with all those hundreds! (of pesos). Then Bart and Diego had to catch the bus, and I had to meet Lisa. So, I checked out the city, I got some comic books in Spanish to read -- "Super Raton" and "Los Amigos de Archi" and "La Pantera Rosa"-- to practice Spanish. It's more fun to practice on fun things, instead of always reading *only textbooks.*

One difference here! Quite a few muchachos were paying attention to me, but I didn't really understand. Every male on the street, on the sidewalks, everywhere, looked at me and made me know they noticed me. They made these noises like, "ch-ch" and whistled at me and were yelling something to me. One boy asked me a question and I said, "No entiendo nada." Good enough.

I finally had a chance to talk to Lisa. She was terrified because of all the guys and the attention they were giving her. (They didn't bother me.) I wonder if they do that to all the girls, or just the Americanas? Cande told us that the guys were looking at us because we are so beautiful. Gracias, señora.

We went on a tour of the city, in a tour bus. We saw different neighborhoods around the city, and it was odd to see their forms of security protection. All the houses have bars on the windows, and the big houses, the mansions, have either high fences with spikes at the top or high (20 feet!) adobe walls with crushed glass embedded in the adobe across the top of the walls.

The tour bus took us all around the city. Something different we saw were the aquaducts, like big, overhead irrigation ditches, to carry water. I couldn't tell if they had water in them, they were up really high, about 20-25 feet above street level, and about 5-10 feet deep. (I took a picture of one.) The rain here is crazy—it rained very hard, poured out of the sky like it was flooding, then the sky cleared, the temperature rose, and all the water dried up in about a half hour; so dry, it didn't even look like it just rained.

Right when one of these raining episodes ended and everything got all dry again, we were still on the tour bus, arriving at Pancho Villa's house, a big villa in the middle of the city, where his widow still lives. Every city in Mexico has a hero, and Pancho Villa is the hero of Chihuahua. I realize he is considered a criminal to United Statesians (they call themselves Americans here, and we are United Statesians) but Sr. Villa is a hero here.

Anyway, we were on the tour, and we went through

Pancho Villa's house. His widow is in her 90's, and she was very nice to us. She talked to us and answered questions. We looked around the house, and I set my purse down on a counter so I could take a picture of the group on the porch. I took the picture, then the bus drove up to pick us up. We all got on and the bus pulled away. Suddenly, a man came running out of Pancho Villa's house with my purse in his hand! He was shouting in Spanish, and the bus driver stopped the bus, and I, feeling like I was dying of embarrassment, went to the front of the bus, got my purse from the man and said with a huge smile, "Gracias." My face felt like it was sticking out about 4 inches.

The city is big, huge. The buildings are painted bright and odd colors, like bright red and turquoise. Most of the buildings are made of adobe, some are made of stone or brick. The roads and streets are in terrible condition, uneven asphalt, if there is even asphalt on them, some are just dirt or maybe adobe. The sidewalks are worse. They look like slabs of concrete in rows, around the edges of the roads. It would be impossible to roller skate on these sidewalks, since no two slabs come together. One slab can stick up two feet off the road and slant at a 45 degree angle, and go under another piece that doesn't even look like it's part of the same sidewalk.

On the brighter side, almost every corner has a park with a fountain in it. There are some beautiful parks and areas, some nice, huge, lovely homes (Sharon is staying with a very rich family with servants, in a mansion), lots of people, very friendly.

On our way home, two guys on a motorcycle (a nice cycle) stopped to talk. They asked me something and I said, "No entiendo mucho." One guy said, "You no speak Spanish?" I said, "Poquito. He asked what we are doing here. I explained that we are students. He was very polite and very handsome! He's not very tall, he's not a big guy like Bart—yes, I could have Bart, if I want a boyfriend. Excuse me, I am not looking for anyone. (Bart pointed out that he and I have all our classes together. Why is Bart always in the back of my mind?)

We went into the house where Cande had lunch ready.

She fed us too much! I hope we are not always required to eat that much. I'll gain a ton!

With our lunch, we had Coca-cola (Coca, they call it), 473 ml. each! In the kitchen is a huge rack of 473 ml. bottles of Coca, where they always keep at least 64 bottles. They also have bottled water in five-gallon jugs, and they don't drink very much water. They use tap water for washing and cleaning and bathing, but not for drinking. They only keep one half gallon of milk in the house at a time. La señora goes to the little corner store every day to get pan y leche (bread and milk). The bread is strange, like sweet rolls with sugar and brown sugar criss-crossed on top. Cande has the neatest bread container, a huge, glass bowl with a glass dome top that goes on it, and she fills it every day with fresh bread that she buys.

Now, I am thinking part in English and part in Spanish. I could write this in Spanish, but I'll keep it in English now and maybe translate the whole thing later.

Cande is really nice. She is always smiling and so eager to do everything for us. We're beginning to speak more Spanish, to communicate with her. This is an experience I'll never forget. I'm very happy these days!

JULY 22, TUESDAY MORNING, 7 A.M.

I want to write about something that happened the other night. I'm not sure why I delayed in writing this, I guess I was going to omit it, forget it, pretend it didn't happen. But it did.

The other night, in El Paso, when everyone else went to the bar, Bart and I went for a walk. We were walking and talking about music and rock bands, and then Bart wanted to change clothes. We had a huge room for all the women, but the men had a small room with three double beds. When we got to his room, Bart suddenly pulled me close to him and kissed me! He tried to nudge me toward the bed, but I backed away. I talked my way out of the bedroom before anything else happened. I wasn't looking for romance, but it found me this time!

I think Lisa is waking up now, and I need to talk to

her. I haven't mentioned "the kiss" to her, or anyone, I just admitted it to myself! But she acts like she already knows. She probably guessed, since I've been spending so much time with Bart.

LATER, THE SAME DAY (TUESDAY)

Today we had our first actual classes, which were OK. I've never been in college before, but it was about the same as high school, only more relaxed and less formal. We had a history class, history of Mexico (what else?). Although I dislike history and usually have a hard time concentrating on it, it seems more interesting when I'm right here, in the country that we're studying. We talked today about Pancho Villa, and we were just at his house yesterday, talking to his widow! I can relate the past to the present. I can see the places we're reading about.

Lisa has been practicing her Spanish constantly with Cande, but I just use Spanish sometimes, when it's really necessary. I am still shy about speaking it, like, I feel like someone will punish me or laugh at me if I pronounce something incorrectly or use the improper grammatical form. I know I need to practice, and I will, I will! Maybe I'm not trying hard enough.

I wrote letters to all my friends and family back home, a million miles and a lifetime away from this wonderful life. I don't want to go back to Los Estados Unidos now, I feel like I could live here forever! I love Mexico! I love this life!

After class, Bart took me to lunch and then he got sick. I walked him home so he could sleep. His "home" is on the poor side of town (ours is in the mid-range, not rich or poor.) His roommate is Diego and they are both staying with a guy named Sergio, who is about their age, and Sergio's mother. All four of them are in a two-room house, and only Sergio's mother has a bed. The guys sleep on bedrolls on the floor of a tiny room. Instead of walls, strands of beads divide the rooms. The place is crowded, dark and cramped, and it smells terrible.

Crystal must have fallen asleep, because she was

83

awakened by voices in the library beneath her.

"What is it? What's wrong?" Rachel asked.

"It's Randall," Pastor Young said.

"What about Randall? Is he all right? Did he get shot?"

"No, he didn't--" Sister Young began.

"Is he dead? He wasn't killed, was he?" Rachel asked, her voice getting higher.

"No, no, he hasn't been killed," Pastor Young said soothingly.

"Then what is it?"

"Vance told us that he is missing," Pastor Young said.

"Missing? What do you mean? How can he be missing?"

"He went on some kind of mission and they haven't heard from him," Pastor Young said.

"Oh, is that all? Then he's okay," Rachel sighed. "If something were wrong, I would feel it."

"We need to keep him in prayer," Pastor Young said.

"I pray for him constantly," Rachel said.

"Don't stop," Pastor Young said.

"Also, Vance is being transferred to the Middle East," Sister Young said.

"Why?" Rachel asked.

"They just decided they needed him over there, I guess," Pastor Young said.

"They wouldn't send him away if his own twin brother were in real trouble," Rachel reasoned.

"I am going to make some calls tomorrow," Pastor Young said, "to see if I can find out anything about Randall. I tried calling this morning, but I couldn't get through. Probably because it's Sunday."

"Don't mention anything to the boys, okay?" Rachel said. "I don't want them to be worried about their father when he's thousands of miles away. They don't need that kind of burden placed on their little minds."

"We won't mention it to them," Sister Young promised. Crystal silently agreed that they wouldn't hear anything from her.

Crystal stayed in her hiding place until after they left. She heard Sister Young in the hall asking Rachel if she had seen her. Rachel checked her room and told her Crystal wasn't in there. The ladies went in the kitchen and Crystal replaced the diary then slipped down the steps. She went into her room, then into the bathroom and purposely made some noise, then she sat on the bed. Rachel poked her head in the doorway.

"Oh, there you are. We were wondering where you were," she said, coming into the room. "Do you want to talk about anything? I'm a really good listener."

Crystal didn't respond. Rachel waited a minute, walking around the room, looking at everything, then she said, "We're going to be eating in a little while, so why don't you wash your hands and you can help me set the table."

Crystal washed her hands and went to the dining room. Rachel showed her where the napkins, plates, glasses and silverware were kept, and Crystal set the table while Sister Young and Rachel chatted. The other kids came tumbling into the house, laughing and joking, and Rachel told them to go wash their hands. Sister Young placed a huge ham in the center of the table and she and Rachel surrounded it with all the trimmings: baked potatoes, dinner rolls, green beans, sweet potatoes, corn and green salads. The family quickly gathered around the table. Pastor Young said a prayer, and they all began to serve themselves and then eat. Crystal sipped her milk and tasted some of the food as the family buzzed around her. She noticed how easily Taylor had changed sides and seemed to be fitting into her new surroundings; but then, Taylor was different. She wasn't like her. Taylor was young and forgetful. Crystal could never forget.

After they ate, Rachel suggested that they all go into the family room to watch a movie on TV. Crystal hadn't watched TV since they had left Tennessee, and she didn't miss it. To avoid confrontation, she followed the others into the family room, and sunk down into one of the small, comfortable chairs. Rachel found a family movie on one of the satellite channels and everyone seemed to enjoy it. Crystal wasn't really paying attention to the program. She had no reason to laugh when the others laughed, or cry with the ladies when they cried. She just sat staring as the images flashed on and off the large screen.

Later, she followed the group as they moved out onto the deck to enjoy the evening. She sat in a lawn chair at the edge of the deck and waited for the evening to end.

CHAPTER 9

On Monday, Crystal didn't awaken until nearly noon. She wandered into the dining room and saw that her place was set with a bowl and spoon, and several boxes of cereal in the middle of the table. Nobody was inside the house, so she poured a little bit of cereal into her bowl and added a small amount of milk from the refrigerator. She ate it and then returned to her big pillow, upstairs in the library. She read more of the diary.

MIERCOLES, EL 23 DE JULIO

We were late for class this morning. The school is within walking distance, only a few blocks from "home", maybe a mile at the most. I'm glad we live so close to the school, because the other students have to ride the bus to school, except Sharon, who has a chauffeur bring her. They all have to get up and go much earlier than we do. It takes us 10 minutes to walk to school.

The school is actually El Instituto Americano de Chihuahua. The building was at one time the governor's mansion. It is similar to most of the buildings in town, but more elegant. We enter through the double doors on the first floor to a type of indoor patio or courtyard, and there are rooms around the perimeter. Our classrooms are upstairs, above the perimeter rooms, with a balcony around the perimeter so the courtyard can be seen from upstairs. The courtyard is actually about two stories high. The whole place is very beautiful.

Lisa and I decided to go for a walk and explore the city after classes today. We went downtown to do some shopping and sightseeing, and we saw Diego, Sergio, Diana and Jane, but we didn't see Bart. Diego said he still isn't feeling well. I wonder if he drank the water? I have tasted some from the tap, but haven't had a full glass. It tastes normal, but I don't want to get sick.

We each have a map of Chihuahua, and we were checking out the city -- and the city was checking us out! Males of all ages, from 4 years old to 94 were noticing us, and letting us know they noticed! They shouted, "Americana, juera!" and "psst-psst" and "chh-chh!" Lisa was embarrassed, but I kind of liked the attention. It was flattering to be noticed by every male in the city, but we pretended not to notice them, as our faces turned all shades of red.

We were checking out the neighborhoods. The architecture is so neat, adobe and stone, and everything seems geometric. Downtown, the buildings are very close together. Most are red-clay color, or light brown or beige or off-white, all the earth tones. Then there are the brightly painted buildings, like turquoise, purple and bright red. All the buildings have steel bars in front of the windows and big, ornately-carved, wooden doors. The stores have cages that close across the front when they're closed, and all the houses have fences around them and bars on the windows. People live in cages here, and need a key to get out! Cande told us earlier that they had been burglarized 3 times, even with all the locks and bars!

Anyway, we were walking around in a loop. I was using my map and I knew exactly where we were and how to get back home, but Lisa thought we were lost. She thought we should go back the way we came, but I had it under control. I was trying not to laugh at her: she was being so over-dramatic! We were on a sidewalk in front of a huge, light brown adobe house with a silver spike fence around it. The houses in the neighborhood were all huge and elegant, with high fences around them and bars in front of all the windows. The yards weren't tended. They were overgrown with dry weeds.

Everything was exciting and funny. We were in a giggly mood, noticing every strange detail and laughing. Lisa kept saying, "Can you believe we are walking around in Mexico? The weather is so beautiful, it all seems so exotic!" We were having a great time, for a couple of hours. Then suddenly she started to panic. "We're going to get lost, and we won't be able to communicate and get back!" Stuck on a city street in Chihuahua, Mexico, forever? No way! I had to keep from laughing, because that just made her panic more, to think

88

that I wasn't being serious. But she was so funny!

In front of the big house, I opened my map and held it against the fence, pointing out to Lisa where we were, which street we were following, where our home was, and how to get there. We weren't more than a mile from home. Lisa was freaking out, and she wouldn't pay attention to what I was saying. She just kept saying we'd never get back and we'd be stuck there and have to live as Mexicans, get jobs and work our way back to the U.S. I kept trying to make her look at the map, but she wouldn't.

The front door of the big house opened and we watched as a tall, beautiful, well-dressed woman with furs, jewels and high heels came down the walkway, which ended about 10 feet to our left, as we faced the house. A small, dark green car with darkened windows drove up to the sidewalk and she got in it. She didn't seem to notice us at all. Lisa whispered, "Are we invisible?" Then a tall, thin man with fuzzy brown hair and glasses, wearing a suit and tie, came out of the house and ran to the car. The window glided down and the man said something to the woman. Then he backed away from the car and it sped away.

I tried to fold up the map without making a scene. (How do you fold a map inconspicuously in a hurry, anyway?) The guy had already noticed us, and he came over to us, smiling. He said his name was Mario, and before I could say anything, Lisa told him we were lost. I started to explain about the map, but he interrupted and invited us into his house. He told us his parents were out of town, on a cruise for a few weeks. Lisa and I silently agreed that it wouldn't hurt us to go inside the house for a few minutes, so we followed Mario into his mansion! The rooms had high ceilings, ornate trim, chandeliers all over the place, fancy tiles and wall paper, and the place was huge! The rooms were all about 20 by 30 feet or so, if not bigger. Mario showed us at least 12 rooms, one with an Olympic size pool! But none of the rooms had any furniture. Then we went into a room that had all the furniture from the entire house crowded into it! There were at least 50 chairs, all different kinds, about 10 beds standing up in a corner, tables, TV's, stereos, kitchen things, sofas, *everything a big house needs in that one room.*

A TV was on across the room. I climbed over some chairs to get close enough to hear the TV, away from the confusing conversation Mario and Lisa were having without me. I sat in a comfortable chair, and I tried to concentrate on the TV. I wasn't understanding the Spanish on the program at all. Unexpected things kept happening. I watched TV for about an hour while Lisa and Mario kept talking, more and more in Spanish.

Right when I was thinking we should leave, Lisa suggested that we go now. I climbed across the chairs again and Mario offered to drive us home. Lisa nodded at me; it was already dark outside. I knew Lisa still thought we were lost, and since we didn't know how safe it was for two teenage American girls to be walking around at night in Chihuahua, we agreed to let Mario drive us home. He wouldn't kidnap us or anything, not after inviting us into his home like this.

So, Mario gave us a ride home, right to Cande and Miguel's house. Lisa and Mario kept talking as we saw the city at night. It's beautiful, with lots of people out walking and standing. I didn't join in their conversation at all. I wasn't in the mood to speak Spanish, or to speak at all. I felt like writing, creating, and I was trying to create a story in my head that I could later write. (By the time I got to paper and pen, I forgot all about the story. Writing this journal is quite enough!)

When Mario stopped in front of our house, he asked us if we wanted to get something to eat. I never eat at that time of evening. I had already had that Coke. But Lisa said she'd go with him. As soon as Cande let me in the house, the car pulled away.

Suddenly I had to speak Spanish. I told Cande that Lisa would be home later. She smiled and asked, "Hungry?" (the one word she knows in English.) I said, "Gracias, no," and came into the bedroom to write. Maybe I should have spent some time with Cande, to get to know her better; but I'm too self-conscious about my Spanish. I guess I can read my Spanish lesson for tomorrow and listen to the radio until Lisa comes home.

I invited Bart to come to our "home" for lunch tomorrow. He's feeling better. Cande is excited about meeting my "novio." I think I hear Lisa coming in now! Goodnight!

24 DE JULIO

Bart came over for lunch and Cande rushed the two of us to the living room while she and her sister, Irma, and Lisa prepared lunch for us. The living room reminds me of 1950's style, with a sofa, an easy chair, a rocking chair, two end tables and a huge, bulky, poorly-working T.V. The color theme is mostly gold, and the sofa sits under a big picture window covered by heavy gold drapes. Bart and I sat on the sofa and we could hear the ladies whispering and giggling in the kitchen. We were talking about the Beatles (again), and suddenly, Bart took my face in his hand and turned it toward his, and kissed me! Lisa made some warning sounds, to let us know they were coming into the living room. Bart is really trying to get me, but so far, it isn't working. I do like him very much, yes, but he can't have me! Freedom is too precious. Anyway, Lisa and Irma carried TV trays with our 7-course lunch, complete with dessert. Cande told us that since Bart was my guest, he and I were to eat first and the other three women would serve us. They returned to the kitchen so we could eat lunch in privacy.

Bart and I ate our lunch. I ate small portions of everything, not too much of anything, even though I liked it all. (Cande makes papas fritas with every meal.) We also had some type of corn beef hash, tortillas, rice, refried beans, soup, plus the main dish, which I can't describe, but it had a corn tortilla in it. It was excellent, and Cande is a master chef! She must've spent the entire morning preparing today's lunch, but she says she does this every day! This was no big deal (no big meal) to her!

After we finished eating and the ladies took our dishes away, Cande and Irma asked Bart a few questions and were impressed by his Spanish. He gave them compliments, laughed and smiled at them, and they both whispered to me that my "novio es muy guapo" (boyfriend is very handsome.) Cande and Irma just sat there, smiling at us, and Bart got shy and invited me for a walk.

We went outside and then, out of the blue, he said he felt sick. He kissed me quickly, then he took off, leaving me standing in front of our house. He ran down the street.

Lisa came outside and asked me what had happened, why did Bart run off like that? Who knows, he's always acting strangely.

1:30 A.M. JULY 25

I can't sleep. I don't know why. I guess I'm just thinking too much. I have known Bart only a week, but it seems like we've been friends all our lives. That is what I would like to remain: friends. Right? Right! I know I can't get involved with anyone. I know I like guys and I love guys, but I have to be free, I have to be me. I can't live for anyone else. I realize this now. It's my life. I have to make the very best of it. Life is what you make it.

This trip is the best experience I've ever had in my life. I feel just great. I'm not depressed, and I haven't been depressed in a long time, not in over a week. That's a nice change. Another good sign is that I've had only one nightmare during this trip so far (instead of 4 or 5 every night.) So, I feel just fine.

I hope Bart doesn't push me to get involved. I just want friend-guys, not a boyfriend.

Sister Young's voice, sounding frantic, brought Crystal back to the present.

"I don't think it's a good idea," she was saying.

"There is no other way," Pastor Young told her.

"But you don't even know where he is."

"Vance showed me. I have a map."

"You don't know any Spanish!"

"God will take care of me. He hasn't brought me this far to leave me."

"I know God will always take care of you, but this could be really dangerous."

"This is *our* boy! He doesn't have any other chance, if

I don't go and get him. The military won't even admit that he's been kidnapped. They say he's a deserter. The rebels will kill him if somebody doesn't go and get him soon. He doesn't have much time before they lose their patience and sacrifice him."

"Why does it have to be you? You have so much here that needs to be done."

"God will take care of everything here, and He will take care of me. Don't worry."

"I know, it's a sin to worry," Sister Young said. "But I am concerned about you."

"Much prayer, what?" Pastor Young asked.

"Much prayer, much power," Sister Young said.

"So just keep praying, and believe that God will answer, like He did when Peter was in jail, and the church was in constant prayer, and the angel opened the prison gates and let Peter out of jail."

"God could do it the same way for Randall," Sister Young suggested.

"He told me that I need to do it this way. He showed me in a dream exactly what I need to do. And He said I need to do it quickly, before it's too late."

"So when are you leaving?"

"I have reservations on a midnight flight tonight."

"Tonight? Do you need us to take you to the airport?"

"I'm going to ask Rachel to take me. She mentioned that she wants to visit her friend in Portland, and this will give her the perfect opportunity. The boys can stay here with you all until she comes back."

They didn't speak for a few moments. Crystal wondered if they had left the room.

"You know I love you?" Sister Young said quietly.

"I know, and I love you," Pastor Young replied.

"I know you'll be careful," she said.

"And prayerful," he agreed. "I should be back in a week or two."

"You always did want to be an ambassador. This is like

your first assignment, secret ambassador to Central America."

"More like secret spy," he teased. They were quiet for another minute or two.

"I'm going to miss you."

"I'll miss you, too."

They left the library. Their conversation confirmed to Crystal that God didn't care at all about anybody. If He did care, would He let Randall be kidnapped? If He did care, would He do something like this, and put Pastor Young in such danger? If He did care, would He make Sister Young so upset? How could a loving God turn His back on people who said they love Him, who trusted Him?

CHAPTER 10

Crystal again escaped into the diary.

SUNDAY, 11:30 A.M., EL 27 DE JULIO
Riding the city bus in Mexico was another experience
that can't be explained, it must be felt. It felt fun and exciting
to me! The fares are so cheap, equivalent to 5-25 cents will
take you anywhere in the city. We went just outside the city
to a huge park, the famous Robinson. The park is fantastic!
I have never seen a park like it in the U.S., or anywhere!
(OK, truthfully, I've never been out of the U.S. until now.)
Robinson is a swimming park with 8 swimming pools. Two
Olympic size pools are in the middle of the park, one pool is
4 feet deep for playing water games like water polo, and the
other is a regular pool with a shallow end, a deep end and
two diving boards. The other pools include a round diving
pool with 3 platforms for diving, two kiddie pools, only about
a foot deep, one round and one rectangle, one half-Olympic
size and two medium size pools.

I dove into the regular Olympic size pool immediately, off
the diving board. I swam 1400 meters, more than a mile! I
felt so good! I missed swimming! I was suddenly energized!
We all watched Diego dive off the top platform several times
(50 meters!) He has a great build and is has decent diving
skills. Jane was especially checking out Diego while Diana
was sunbathing (trying to get a tan through layers of make-
up). I challenged Diego to a 100 meter race, and I kept up
with him. He just barely beat me.

We all played a game of water polo with a bunch of people,
including some of the lifeguards, who initiated the game. If
their job is to keep people happy at the park, they were doing
it well. It was a blast, splashing and jumping and swimming
and bumping.

After we got tired of water polo, two of the lifeguards
asked Lisa and me to join them in the diving pool, to practice
diving. We said no, thanks, but we had a great time watching
them. They were diving beautifully, like professionals, swan
dives off the top platform, twists and flips and doubles and

triples and backs and rolls and dives. Everyone at the park stopped what they were doing to watch the two handsome men dive. They were so awesome!

When they finished diving practice (it's true, practice makes perfect) I challenged the cutest lifeguard to a race. He flashed me the brightest smile and said sure! He also beat me, but only by about a meter. (Not bad for a GIRL, huh?) Lisa had gone to join a volley ball game, and the other lifeguard had disappeared, so that left me alone with Mr. Wonderful. We started talking, mostly in Spanish. Then he spoke English while I spoke Spanish. His name is Dany, with one "n" and the other guy that was diving with him is his brother, Manuel. Dany was on the Mexican volleyball team in the last Olympics! No wonder he looked so familiar, I probably saw him on TV! Now he is training to be on the diving team in the next Olympics. Wow! That's so amazing! I was truly impressed. He is tall, a little over 6 feet, with medium brown hair, clear, blue eyes, a mustache and an incredible lifeguard's tan. He asked for our phone number and said he'd call me at 7:30!

Lisa also met a guy at the park, Hugo. They met playing volleyball and stayed together the whole time Dany and I were together, so we didn't get to compare notes about our new friends before we left the park. Hugo is kind of cute, but not at all as gorgeous as Dany! Hugo kissed Lisa's cheek as she was boarding the city bus, how sweet!

When it was time to go, I went home with Diego to visit Bart. Poor Bart, he was really sick. He looked terrible. He hadn't listened to his new Beatles album yet. It was still sealed. He grabbed my arm and the album and pulled me over to the stereo. He ripped open the wrapper and removed it from the album cover, then took the album out and put it gently on the turntable.

"You should always remove the cellophane immediately after opening it," he told me, "because when it gets hot, the album can sweat and warp if the wrapper is still on it." I didn't know that.

"This is a first edition of this album-- not available in the states. This is great." He was smiling. He looked so excited.

He lowered the needle onto the first track.

"I always look forward to getting a new album so I can do this. Don't you love doing this?"

"Doing what? Playing it for the first time?"

"No, checking each track." He let the record play for a couple of seconds then lifted the needle and moved it to the second track, let it play for a few seconds then lifted the needle again, and so on, until he had heard a few seconds of each song on the first side. Then he flipped the album over and did the same thing to side two.

"I have never done that," I confessed. "I always put the needle at the beginning of the side I like best, let that side play, and then turn the record over and listen to the other side."

Bart looked at me as if I'd said I like to take my evening walk on the moon.

"Really?" he asked, as if it were impossible for him to believe that I did such a thing.

We listened to the album and talked for a long time. In the middle of a conversation about our Spanish class, Bart got up, walked across the room and looked straight at me.

"Isn't it strange to think that we are both going to marry someone else?" he asked. Very strange to think that. Why were we thinking that? What had brought that up? I told him about Dany and I said that since Bart was sick, I had made other plans for Saturday night.

"Of course, you wouldn't want to wait at home while I was sick, would you?"

"Of course not. You are free to see anyone you want to see."

He didn't seem to take me seriously. Singing, he told me to do whatever I want to do. I'm glad he put it that way! I guess I expected him to get mad and tell me not to go, then I'd tell him he couldn't tell me what to do, then I wouldn't feel guilty about going out with Dany. Did I feel guilty?

Bart said he needed to take a nap, so I walked back home. Lisa was waiting for me. She was wondering if it was too soon to date guys we just met the same day, then we decided that here in Mexico we can't go by standards that ruled us in the U.S. Everything and everyone was too different. I told Lisa all about Dany. She says she's in love with him! I barely noticed Hugo, but Lisa sure noticed Dany.

Lisa asked me, "What about Bart?"

"What about Bart?" I answered. Another reason to laugh hysterically.

At exactly 7:30, the phone rang. Dany invited me to his birthday party. Lisa got my camera ready to take a picture of us.

"He's so beautiful," she giggled, "you have to preserve this moment in a picture." More giggles, both of us.

The doorbell rang at exactly 8:00. Cande spoke with Dany for a minute in Spanish, so rapidly that I didn't catch anything they said. She whispered to me that he's "muy guapo," and I was still grinning from that when Lisa snapped our picture. I know that's one photo that will turn out -- Dany looks like a model!

His car is a black VW, all fixed up, with mag wheels, a beautiful, spotless, gray interior, an excellent stereo, and a musical horn! Musical horns are very popular here, in Chihuahua, and they play an endless number of tunes, some up to 30 seconds long! They are kind of neat, but I can see how quickly the novelty could wear off.

We got into the car and drove 4 blocks down the street, and the car died. Dany asked me to drive while he pushed. Here I am, driving in Mexico! Luckily, we were on a downhill slant. The car started on the first try and Dany jumped back in. He drove to his house, where I met his mother, sister and father. Dany's sister served a cake that she had made, then they all sang songs in Spanish. The whole family was very nice to me, and I had fun. I still felt shy using Spanish, but they all seemed to understand me, so I guess the few sentences I managed to spit out were OK.

The party was fun and short. Dany said he wanted to show me the beauty of his city, so we went for a ride. We got into the comfortable little car and drove silently up into the hills around Chihuahua. We could see all the lights of the city, and it was truly a majestic sight. It looked so far away, so quiet. We parked in a very secluded place, up on a *hill, away from everyone and everything. We got out of the car and looked up at the sky, the romantic, persuasive sky. I felt a warm feeling come over me, chills ran up and down my spine. My heart was racing. I had never felt like that before, but I maintained my composure.*

I was feeling so good and I was swept away by his good looks, muscular body and irresistible charm. He sang me a love song in Spanish while I melted into the surrealism of the night. He was looking into my eyes, making me feel as if I were the only woman on earth. When he finished singing, he turned on the car stereo. The song "Daniel" by Elton John came on, and Dany pulled me close to him and put this arm around me.

"Whenever you hear this song, think of me," he whispered, looking deeply into my eyes.

"I will," I promised, knowing that I always will.

He held me close to him and asked me if I wanted him to be my novio. He said he'd like to be. I couldn't answer.

He was so romantic, the whole experience was like a wonderful dream. He got me home before midnight, which gave him extra points with Mom. Even though Mom isn't here, her spirit is, telling me to get home on time when I'm out with a guy. Yes, Mom.

Time to go. Cande has lunch ready. Lisa's anxious for Mario's call. I may go see Bart today. I'll call him after we eat. Today will be a good day to relax.

Crystal put away the diary and sat for awhile, thinking about the author and still wondering if it were true, or just a story that someone had created. She gazed out the window for a few minutes and was startled to hear Taylor speaking, standing right beside her.

"What are you doing?" she asked. Crystal's heart jumped, but she continued to stare out the window.

"How long have you been sitting here?" Taylor asked. "Well, you can just waste your whole life away, if that's what you want to do." She padded down the steps without waiting for Crystal to respond.

In the evening, Rachel left to drive Pastor Young to the Portland airport. The other kids didn't know anything about the real reason they went to the city. They were told that he was going to take care of some business, and Rachel was going to visit her friend in Portland for a couple of days, which was all true, but the details of his mission were missing. The kids watched another movie in the family room, while eating popcorn and drinking fruit punch. Crystal again tuned out the movie while she waited for it to end.

Later that night, after they had gone to bed, Crystal heard a strange crying, like a moaning sound. The moonlight was streaming in through an opening in the curtains. She looked over at Taylor, who was sound asleep, then stepped out into the hallway. The sound was coming from the living room, where she found Sister Young kneeling at the altar and praying. She was crying out to God, praying for the safety of her son and her husband. Crystal wanted to tell her she was just wasting her time, God wasn't listening and He wouldn't help her, but if that was what Sister Young chose to do, Crystal wasn't about to stop her. She returned to the bedroom and quietly closed the door.

CHAPTER 11

The next morning Sister Young awakened Crystal and Taylor early.

"Come on, girls, let's go on that shopping trip I promised you last week," she said as they slowly began to move about in their beds. "We'll see if the boys want to go with us, but I doubt they will. They can go shopping any time with their mother. I'm sure they'll prefer to go play at Ronnie's farm."

They got dressed and went to the dining room table, where Kenny and Keith were already eating breakfast. Crystal and Taylor poured themselves some cereal and milk.

"Do you boys want to go shopping with us?" Sister Young asked. "We need to go to the mall to get some clothes for the girls."

"Shopping! Yuk!" Kenny said, disgusted.

"Shopping for clothes? At a mall?" Keith asked. "Booooor-ing!"

"Can we go to Ronnie's farm?" Kenny asked. "He said he has a new horse, AND his other horse had a baby colt last month! He said we can come over any time."

"I think that's a great idea," Sister Young said. "I'll call his mother and let her know you are coming. We can drop you off when we leave."

"No, thank you, we can walk," Keith said.

"Yes, ma'am, we can walk," Kenny said. "It's not that far."

"Yeah, we need the exercise," Keith said. "That's what Mom always says, that we need to burn off all that energy."

"She's right about that," Sister Young said.

The boys finished their cereal, put their dishes in the dishwasher and flew out the door. Crystal and Taylor also put their dishes in the dishwasher and followed Sister Young to the garage and the small red car. Crystal got in the back seat to let Taylor engage in conversation with Sister Young.

"Hmmm, I wonder if we should go to Yakima or to the Tri-Cities mall?" Sister Young asked. "Let's go to Yakima.

I can pick up some other things we need while we're there. When we go shopping, we get what we need for a whole month. We don't go into town every day, like some people, or even every week, and certain things we can only get when we go to the city. We can't get everything we need in Goldendale. The town is just too small to have everything."

Crystal stared out the window while Sister Young kept talking. They drove through forests, up higher in the hills, then down a big hill, through more forests, and through a huge valley where the trees suddenly stopped. She saw wild horses grazing all over the hills on the sides of the valley. They drove through a town with murals painted on many of the buildings, then through another valley. She wasn't listening to anything Sister Young was saying.

They finally arrived at the mall and went into a store. Crystal hadn't been to a mall before, and she had never been inside a fancy department store like this one. They made their way to the girls' department and Sister Young asked them what kind of clothes they liked. Crystal didn't care anything about her clothes; she didn't know why they needed to buy anything new. What did a person's life have to do with the clothes she wore? She thought that Sister Young was just wasting her money. Taylor seemed to be enjoying the shopping spree, and Sister Young seemed to be having a good time as well. Had she already forgotten that her husband was on a dangerous mission? She didn't seem to be worried or thinking about him at all.

Since Crystal wasn't responding, Sister Young suggested that Taylor select some clothes for her sister as well as for herself. Taylor found two sets of matching shorts and tops and swimming suits for each of them. Sister Young told Taylor to also choose a couple of dresses for each of them, and some long pants, some sandals and some underclothes. Taylor found some more shorts and shirts she liked, and a pair of shoes. Sister Young bought everything Taylor put in the basket. They left the store with several bags of clothes and shoes, and put them all in the trunk of the car, then they went back into the mall and Sister Young bought some things she needed. Crystal wasn't paying attention to where they were going or what she was buying. She did notice a variety of shops in the mall, and she saw lots of teenagers standing around in different places. She wondered what they were doing, and she hoped they didn't notice that she looked different from them. They didn't seem to be noticing her at all, they were involved in their own lives.

After Sister Young purchased everything she needed for the farm, she took Crystal and Taylor to a place called a Food Court to eat. She asked them what kind of food they wanted; they could choose from hamburgers, Greek food, Chinese food, sub sandwiches, Mexican food or hot dogs. None of the choices sounded good or bad to Crystal. Her appetite and her desire for food had died months ago, when her father died. Taylor suggested Greek food, since they had never tried it. Crystal picked at the weird, fat tortilla-type bread and the spicy meat inside and ate a couple of the tomatoes while Taylor kept saying how delicious it was.

When they were finished shopping, they returned to the car and drove back to the farm. Crystal stared out the window the whole time, not listening to the conversation in the front seat. A few minutes after they arrived, the twins came running into the house, panting.

"I beat you!" a twin said, between breaths.

"No, I beat you!"

"Did not!"

"Did too!"

"You can't beat me!"

"I did!"

"No way! You'll never beat me!"

"Did too!"

"Did not!"

"Boys," Sister Young said sternly. "That's enough."

"Sorry, Grandma," they said together.

"Hey, what d'ya get at the store? Anything good to eat?"

"We didn't go shopping for food, but we have plenty of

food. What do you want?"

"Cookies!"

"Did you eat some lunch?"

"We had sandwiches."

"Yeah, about 10 hours ago."

"We weren't gone for 10 hours."

"Seems like it."

"Seems like 10 days."

"Did not!"

"Did too!"

"Boys?"

"Sorry, Grandma," they said.

"You can't just keep doing the same thing and then telling me you're sorry. You are not acting like you are sorry. If you really are sorry, don't do it again."

"We won't."

"Do you promise?"

"We promise."

"You promise what?"

"We won't do it any more."

"You won't do what?"

"Ummm..." Kenny said.

"What you don't want us to do," Keith said.

"Don't argue. Please don't argue with each other," she said kindly.

"Yes, ma'am," they said, hanging their heads.

"Hey, when is Mom coming back?" Keith asked.

"Either tomorrow or the next day," Sister Young said.

"Then do we have to leave?" Keith asked.

"Do you want to leave?" Sister Young asked.

"No, we want to stay all summer!" Kenny said.

"You can stay as long as your mother wants you to stay."

"Oh, man!"

"She won't let us stay all summer."

"You know you can come here any time," Sister Young told them.

"Hey, Grandma, can we go swimming in the pond?"

"It's not really clean enough for swimming," she said, "but you can go in the hot tub."

"Yeah! Hot tub!" they shouted.

"Go find your swimming trunks," Sister Young said. "Crystal and Taylor, you can go in too, you have new swim suits. It's big enough for all of us. I think I'll go in for awhile with you. It'll be relaxing."

Crystal went to her room but didn't put on her new swimming suit. She sat on the bed while Taylor changed and then joined the others in the hot tub in the back yard. Crystal sneaked up the steps in the library and took out the diary again.

MIERCOLES, EL 30 DE JULIO

Now it's 7:30 a.m. Yesterday we went swimming at Robinson, and we saw Manuel, but not Dany. We had a good time anyway, but I would like to see Dany again. Manuel invited Lisa and me to his house for dinner, and we accepted the invitation. We ate a huge meal at their house and again I saw their mother and sister. They smiled at us and I felt kind of out of place without Dany there, but we got through the 7-course meal in a hurry. Manuel offered to drive us home, and right then Dany came home. He came with Manuel to drive us home. Lisa and Manuel rode in front and Dany and I rode in back, and he wrapped his arms around me and whispered into my ear that he missed me and wanted to go out with me again. We decided to make it a double date with Manuel and Lisa. They were getting along quite well, laughing about something or other most of the time. It was wonderful riding in the back and having Dany hold me and whisper to me. He sent tingles down my spine!

Too soon the ride was over and Dany kissed me gently and said he'd call at 8:00 tomorrow night (tonight, now) to set the date. Muy bien, adios para ahora. Sounds good to me!

The writer of the diary seemed sincere. Crystal thought it could have really happened, but what had happened to Bart and Dany and Lisa? This couldn't possibly be Sister Young's writing, could it? Thirty years ago, could she have been 17? Did she know how to speak Spanish? If Sister Young hadn't written it, who had? Was this a fictional story?

Maybe somebody had purchased the diary. Crystal examined the book to see if the ink looked authentic. It was beginning to fade in places, but she couldn't really tell. She had read diaries in the library at her school, and they were printed to look like they were handwritten.

She put the diary back into its hiding place and wandered downstairs into the library. As she was about to go back to her room, she noticed a shelf near the door with several books written by Claire Young. They were real books like the ones in stores and libraries. She picked up the nearest one titled *The Organized Pastor's Wife* and thumbed through it. She picked up the next one, *Weekends with Dad,* and the next one, *Closer to Mom than Ever Before*. They looked like nonfiction books. She found several poetry books and some kind of health book, all written by Claire Young.

So Sister Young was a writer, but none of these books were fiction. The diary had to be fiction; it was too far-fetched to be true, and that writer was not anything like Sister Young.

Crystal replaced the books and went to her room. She stretched out and waited for sleep to overtake her, so she could stop thinking for awhile. She didn't need any dinner. She could just rest for a couple of days and not listen to anyone or do anything. Nothing was important to her, and the reading and thinking she had done this evening had exhausted her.

CHAPTER 12

The next morning, Sister Young encouraged Crystal to walk with her around the perimeter of the property. She said something about the fresh air and exercise helping her to feel better. Crystal walked the entire distance with Sister Young but she didn't feel any better when they finished. Her legs felt tired, though, and she decided to take a nap in the early afternoon.

Crystal was awakened by Rachel's voice, calling everyone to come and watch the news on TV with her. Crystal pulled herself out of bed, the muscles in her legs feeling sore as she joined the others, who were gathered in front of the TV in the family room.

"My friend, Karen," Rachel said excitedly, "just got a job with the National News Network, and her first story is going to be on in just a few minutes. I visited her mother when I was in Portland, and she told me Karen just got the job in New York! She moved there a few days ago. She always wanted to be a reporter. She was working in a TV station in Portland for a few months, then she had an interview in New York, and they hired her on the spot. Oh, shhhh! I think this is it."

An announcer sitting at a desk said, "We would like to begin our special segment on health today, and we have a new reporter who just joined us, all the way from Portland, Oregon. She is asking people on the streets of New York an interesting question: would you eat poison, if it tasted good? Let's see how people responded to our new features reporter, Karen Daly, today."

The scene changed to show a young woman with a microphone standing on a sidewalk in New York City. She approached a young man.

"Would you eat poison, if it tasted good?" she asked.

"No way!" he shouted, at her, and walked away.

She stopped an older woman. "Would you eat poison, if it tasted good?" she asked.

"Poison? No, I would never eat poison," the lady answered.

"Would you eat poison, if it tasted good?" she asked another man.

"No, I wouldn't eat poison, even if it did taste good," he said.

"Would you eat poison, if it tasted good?" she asked a middle-aged woman.

"Well, I wouldn't intentionally eat poison, but I think some of the things we eat today are poison in disguise" she said, looking into Karen's eyes.

"She could be onto something," Karen said to the camera. "Today, I interviewed naturalistic health expert, Marilyn Monsoon, who says most Americans eat plenty of poison every day, without even knowing it, just because it tastes good."

The scene changed to show Karen sitting with a lady at a table. Crystal noticed that the other lady, in contrast to Karen's fair skin and blonde hair, had golden brown skin like her own, and thick, black hair. She was very beautiful; and even without any makeup, her skin was flawless.

"I'm here with Marilyn Monsoon, who has done extensive studies on what we eat and how it affects us. Marilyn, what is the poison that most Americans eat every day?"

"Well, Karen, that poison is sugar," Marilyn answered. "Most Americans eat a lot of sugar, much more sugar than they are aware they are eating. They don't realize they are eating poison, because it tastes so good."

"Sugar is practically one of the food groups in America. Why do you call it poison?"

"Because that's what it is. Poison is something deadly or toxic to our bodies, and that's what sugar is. Any dentist will tell you that sugar can dissolve teeth. But most doctors won't tell you what a terrible effect sugar has on our bodies."

"Can you explain what you mean by that?"

"Lots of people think that sugar boosts their energy, but really sugar slows a person down. Sugar is not easy for the body to digest, so the body has to work harder to break it down and to eliminate it. Sugar basically bogs down all the systems of the body. Really, sugar puts a body under attack. The body is at war with the sugar, drawing energy away from its essential functions. The more sugar a person eats, the harder the body has to work."

"But we don't really see that happening, do we? Is that something that happens and we never know about it? How is that like poison?"

"It's a slow poison, killing us slowly. Too much sugar over a long period of time can cause a multitude of problems, including diabetes. Diabetes can lead to blindness, amputations, a diabetic coma, and even death. Would you eat a food that said on the label, 'eating this can lead to blindness, amputations, a coma or death,' Karen?"

"Well, no, but I'm not diabetic."

"Maybe right now you aren't. But that doesn't mean you won't become diabetic. Many people today have diabetes but don't know it yet. Why do you think we have such a huge increase in diabetes in this country today? It has become a personal choice, a lifestyle choice, to greatly increase sugar intake and at the same time reduce physical activity. That is really a deadly combination."

"What about people who aren't diabetic? Is sugar really that bad for us?"

"Yes, it is. Like I mentioned earlier, sugar causes all your systems in your body to work harder, so the body can't take care of the essential functions efficiently. Another thing about sugar is that cancer feeds on sugar. If a person has cancer, and that person continues to eat sugar, that cancer will spread and grow, because sugar is the nutrition it needs."

"I've never heard about that."

"Most people haven't. It's not widely publicized, and the reason is that it is too simple a solution: money. Do you know how many people make their living around the disease of cancer? A partial list includes doctors and specialists and people working in nursing homes and hospitals and clinics. Our American economy is based around the sale of sugar. Do you realize that our economy would essentially collapse if all

Americans stopped eating sugar?"

"How can you say that?"

"Well, think about it. Think about the American diet. Soda pop. sugary breakfast cereals, donuts, muffins, coffee with sugar, specialty coffees, pancakes with sugary syrup, most canned foods, including many vegetables, have added sugar, most breads are made with sugar, even peanut butter and French fries often have sugar added."

"French fries have sugar added?"

"Yes, many of the fast food establishments add sugar to their French fries to make them taste better. When you start reading the labels, you will be surprised to see how much of the food you eat contains sugar, and contains a lot of sugar. A bottle of soda pop might contain 8 to 21 teaspoons of sugar. Can you imagine that? If you add three spoonfuls of sugar to a cup of tea or a cup of coffee, it makes your drink so sweet. What if you were to add 21 spoons of sugar to your coffee? Then you would have the same amount of sugar as in just one bottle of some kinds of soda pop. I have seen people drinking those super-size cups of pop, or drinking one bottle after another, literally pouring cups of excess sugar into their bodies, day after day, just in the soda pop they drink. I was noticing the other day, a sad commentary on our American system, when I noticed two vending machines side-by-side, a pop machine and a vending machine with bottles of water. A bottle of soda pop was only $.50, while a bottle of water was $1.25. So what do you think most people will buy, given those two choices?"

"Most people would probably buy two bottles of pop for a dollar, instead of one bottle of water for $1.25," Karen reasoned.

"That's right. Another thing about sugar is that it is addictive. Eating sugar makes a person want to eat more sugar. Once you get that taste in your mouth, you want more, and it's hard to break the sugar habit. It isn't easy. It takes effort to look for foods that specifically don't have any sugar, and those foods are not always easy to find. I'm not talking about foods that have sugar substitutes; that is a subject for another time, foods we eat that are not real foods.

"So back to your original question Karen, would people eat poison, if it tasted good? Yes, they do, pounds and pounds of poison in the form of sugar every year. People tend to think of sugar as being candy bars, cookies, cakes, brownies, ice cream, frosting, sweets and things like that. Don't get me wrong, those items do have a high concentration of sugar. If people would stop eating just those things, eliminate all of those items from their diets, they would be a lot healthier. But to really eliminate sugar from your diet, all sugar, you need to read the labels, because sugar is added to so many other foods these days."

"Marilyn, I just went to the doctor last week, and she didn't mention anything about eliminating sugar from my diet or even cutting down on sugar. If there is such a health benefit to not eating sugar, why aren't doctors telling their patients to avoid eating sugar?"

"That depends on what kind of doctor you have and what your doctor really wants from you. Does your doctor really want you to get better, or does he want you to keep coming back to him? You have to be aware that many doctors were put through medical school on scholarships provided by pharmaceutical companies. Many doctors feel they have an obligation to support those drug companies, by prescribing medication to their patients. If you found out you were a borderline diabetic, who would benefit if you stopped eating sugar? Only you would benefit, because your health would improve. You would have no need for any type of maintenance medication. But if your doctor prescribed medication, he would benefit because you would have to keep coming back to see him, to have your levels monitored, and the drug companies would benefit, because you would have to keep buying the medication for the rest of your life. So there's a whole cycle involved. Karen, I'm sure this is not going to be a very popular report."

"I believe you are right, Marilyn, but it is my job to help

the public become aware of controversial issues, so that they can make choices for themselves. We are out of time now, but I would like to interview you again soon on some of the other health issues you would like to discuss."

"Thank you, Karen," Marilyn said.

Karen turned to face the camera. "Thank you, Marilyn Monsoon, naturalistic health expert. For National News Network, I'm Karen Daly."

Rachel turned down the volume on the TV with the remote control.

"That's not really true, is it, Mom?" Kenny asked. "Sugar isn't really poison, is it?"

"I guess some people think it is," Rachel said.

"Do we have to stop eating candy and stuff?" Keith asked.

"Well, I think it would be a good idea if we cut down," Rachel said.

"I agree," Sister Young said. "We don't eat a lot of sugar here, but we are able to control it better than most people, because we grow our own food and cook all of our meals, so we know exactly what we are eating. Usually when I bake a cake or make cookies, I use honey or molasses instead of sugar."

"Mom, was that your friend Karen on TV?" Kenny asked.

"That's Karen," Rachel said.

"She sure has grown," Sister Young remarked.

"Well," Rachel said. "you probably haven't seen her in at least ten or twelve years.

"That's true. She was just a teenager last time I saw her. You know, even then she wanted to be a reporter. She interviewed me a few times for her class projects."

"I think her topic today will probably make a few people mad," Rachel said.

"Well, how many people do you think watch this channel? And how many are watching at this time of day? And of those who watch it, how many will believe what that Monsoon lady said?" Sister Young asked.

"It only takes one famous person to notice and make a fuss over it, and it can become a big controversy," Rachel said.

"That's true," Sister Young said. "But a friend of mine told me some of these same things years ago, and I haven't seen even the tiniest decline in the use or sales of sugar, although I did cut down on our purchase and use of sugar in this house."

"Well, your friend just didn't have the publicity that Karen can give a person. She will make sure the story is well known," Rachel said.

"Can we be excused now?" Kenny asked.

"Yes, you may," Rachel said.

"We're going outside!" Keith said.

"Dinner will be ready in about an hour," Rachel told them, as they were going out the door.

"Crystal, I think it would be a good idea if you go outside a little more often," Sister Young said. "I really enjoyed our walk this morning. I would like you to either take a walk or ride one of the bikes every morning, to get some fresh air and exercise. It will help you feel better. Will you do that for me?"

Crystal didn't respond.

"I'll take that as a 'yes,' then," Sister Young said. "You don't have to go outside right now, but you can go out any time you want."

Crystal didn't want to do anything. It really made no difference to her if she sat in this room with Rachel and Sister Young, if she sat in the room alone, if she went outside and sat in a chair, or if she went to her room and sat on the bed. Her own life was of no concern to her. The only thing that even slightly held her interest was the life in the diary. The writer was young, yet bold, and she was not afraid to let herself get into new and different situations. She seemed to know what to say and when not to talk, in English and also in Spanish. She knew how to make friends out of strangers. She seemed so happy with her life. She was really living.

"Rachel, can you and the boys stay here with us for a few more days?" Sister Young asked. "I need some help around the farm. I have a couple of neighbors I can ask for help, but if you can just give me a hand with some of the daily things I need to do, I would really appreciate it."

"Sure, we can stay for a week or two. Everything at home will be fine," Rachel said.

"That's great! The boys seem to be enjoying themselves."

"They always do when we're here. They were asking if they could stay all summer, but I don't want to do that to you."

"If you want to leave them here for awhile, feel free. I have plenty of room, and plenty of time, and plenty of chores for them to do."

"We'll talk about it," Rachel said.

Rachel and Sister Young left the room and Crystal sat in the chair for a few minutes. She didn't have anything to do, and she didn't want to do anything. Rachel came back in the room.

"Do you want to talk about anything?" Rachel asked. "I'm really concerned about you, Crystal, because you seem really depressed."

That description didn't really surprise Crystal, because she had heard it before, but she didn't feel depressed. She didn't feel anything.

"What do you like to do?" Rachel asked. "What is your favorite subject in school? I always liked art. That was my favorite subject. I love to draw and paint and work with clay. I loved all types of visual art. I'm not really a good artist, but it is my passion. I love art and I love to work with art. Since I'm not that good, I decided to become an art teacher so I could share my passion with other people, and, hopefully, inspire kids to love art too. Do you like art?"

Crystal had failed at every art form she had tried; she didn't like art. She remembered one time she wanted to paint a picture in class, but her hands couldn't do what her mind wanted them to do. The colors were off, the shapes were distorted, and the beautiful scene in her mind just didn't transfer onto the paper. The whole process was much harder than it looked, harder than she imagined it would be. In her art class, her lump of clay never progressed beyond a lump – again, her hands couldn't shape it the way she wanted it to look. Crystal did not like art; it did not behave for her.

"Well, do you like to write? Writing can be a form of art. You can actually paint a picture using words. When you see a scene in your mind, you can describe that scene in such detail, like an artist uses a brush. Or maybe you are not a visual type person. Me, I see pictures in my head, but some people see words or even numbers and graphs and other things. Like if someone says the word 'cat,' what do you see? I see a picture of a cat in my head. But I have a friend who, when someone says 'cat,' she sees the word 'cat' typed or written out, c-a-t, before she sees a picture of a cat. One of my other friends is such a word-type person, if I say a number, like 6, she will see the word spelled out first, 'six,' then she will see the number 6, and then she will see six items, usually two columns of three. Isn't that weird? Or maybe it doesn't seem weird to you, but I'm just saying that everyone is different, with different styles and different interests. So, what do you like? What does Crystal like to do?"

Crystal didn't like anything, she had no interest in anything. She didn't say anything.

"You know, Jesus can help you," Rachel said. "If you don't want to talk to anyone, you can talk to Jesus without even opening your mouth. He knows what is in your heart. He knows what is in your mind. He knows what you are going to think, even before you think it. He wants to be your Friend, and He is a Friend who will never leave you. He doesn't want you to be depressed. He cares about you. He doesn't want you to be alone, or to go through anything alone. He wants to comfort you. Do you know Him as your personal Savior?"

Crystal didn't answer. She did not believe what Rachel was saying, because she knew that Jesus did not care about her. If He did care, He wouldn't have let Daddy die. He wasn't thinking about how she felt then, so why would He care about her now?

"I know you have been really suffering," Rachel said, "but you have to let go of your suffering and let God heal your wounds. I know He can do it, because He did it for me. You are not the only person who has lost someone you love. I did, too. I lost my little brother, Matthew. When I was 10 and he was 8, our family went to the lake for a picnic. After we ate, we were playing with some other kids in the water. There were lots of kids there, and I wasn't really watching Matt, I was playing with some other girls on the tire swing. One of the boys ran over and said a boy was just floating in the water, so we all ran over there, and it was Matt. A bigger boy pulled him out and tried to revive him, but he was dead. He had drowned, right there. We were having a great picnic, and then my brother died.

"In a way, I felt like it was my fault, because I should have been watching him, but everyone kept telling me, it wasn't my fault. I felt so bad, so guilty, until one Sunday at church, the pastor prayed for me and told me to give all my guilt to God. I apologized to my parents, but they told me they didn't blame me. Then the whole church prayed for me, and I felt my burden lift from me. I knew that if it wasn't my fault, then I was okay, and if it was my fault, I was forgiven. Nobody is perfect, but God still loves us anyway. When you refuse to let God in, you are really punishing yourself."

Crystal knew that God was punishing her, and He would always be punishing her. It *was* her fault Daddy had killed himself, and nothing would ever bring him back to life. He was gone forever, and it was all her fault. She didn't need to talk to anybody about it, or about anything else.

"Come on, let's go outside. We'll go in the woods, where it isn't too hot," Rachel said.

Crystal followed her outside. They walked up the trail into the woods, toward the Back 40.

"Have you been here before?" Rachel asked. "This is like a magical place. I was so excited when I heard that Dad and Claire bought this other piece of property."

They walked through the woods and stopped at the overlook. Rachel took Crystal to a big rock that was shaded by the trees and motioned for her to sit on it, then Rachel sat beside her. Crystal looked down at the ponds and clearings between the trees.

"What do you think of this place?" Rachel whispered. "I would love to paint it. Of course, nobody can duplicate the glorious scenes that God has made for us to enjoy, but this could make a nice series of paintings. You know, have you ever thought about why God made earth in color, instead of just black and white? I think He made colors just for us to enjoy."

They sat in silence for a long time. Crystal's imagination began to flicker, and she thought she could almost see fairies and gremlins and miniature kings and queens and princesses, riding on dragonflies and gathering in one of the clearings near a pond. She began to imagine a life going on right next door, practically, an unseen life of tiny people. Her mind began to drift as she thought about how they lived in tiny houses hidden in the woods or under the ground, taming small animals to use as beasts of burden. She imagined a different type of language that even the animals could understand.

She came to herself. She was sitting on a rock beside Rachel, and there were no such things as fairies or tiny civilizations. She was living among strangers and did not care about anything. Her sister had betrayed her and her daddy would never come back.

"This is like a magical place," Rachel repeated. "I almost feel like I am under a spell when I look down there and let my imagination wander. All the fairy tales that were ever written must have been imagined right down there. Don't you just love it here?"

Crystal did not want to admit, even to herself, that she had felt the same way, that she enjoyed this spot. She did not deserve to let her mind wander, or to let her imagination carry her to another world. The present and her suffering were her continual burden.

117

"Let's go back to the house," Rachel said. "Sister Young probably has dinner ready for us." They returned to the house and to another home-cooked meal. Taylor was acting like a sister to the twins, jabbering and playing and having fun with them. Crystal realized that she would need to forever carry her burden alone.

CHAPTER 13

Rachel and her boys stayed at the farm for three more weeks. Every day, Rachel talked to Crystal and walked with her to the Back 40 overlook. Several evenings they all went upstairs to the library tower to look at the stars and the moon, and every Sunday, they all went to church. A visiting pastor came to preach, but Crystal tuned him out and didn't hear a word he said.

At the end of June, Rachel and the twins went back home, promising to come back soon. Crystal didn't know where they lived, but it wasn't important. Their place of residence made no difference to her.

After Rachel and the twins left, Taylor began to spend a lot of her time with Sister Young. They worked in the kitchen together, took care of the animals together, and helped neighbors who came to work in different areas of the farm. Sister Young gave Crystal two chores: to vacuum the house once a week and to dust in certain rooms twice a week. Crystal did her chores with precision, but without enthusiasm. She refused to talk even to Taylor when they were alone. While Rachel was still there, Crystal hadn't been able to read any more of the diary, because Rachel seemed to be either watching Crystal or guarding the library most of the time. Crystal wondered if the diary could be hers, but then remembered that it had been written in 1975, and Rachel probably hadn't even been born then. She wondered if Rachel knew about the diary.

On Sunday before the 4th of July, Sister Young announced at church that they wouldn't be having the annual 4th of July picnic at their house, since Pastor Young still was not back from his missionary trip. She hadn't told the church members exactly what he was doing – as a matter of fact, Crystal thought, she was the only one beside Sister Young who really knew where Pastor Young had gone and what he was doing. They hadn't heard anything from him since he left. Sister Young asked the whole church to pray for Pastor Young and his safe return. Crystal knew it wouldn't do any good, because God had stopped answering prayers a long time ago, but the rest of the church members acted like they believed their prayers would make a difference.

One night the next week, after everyone had gone to bed, Crystal sneaked up to the library loft and pulled out the diary again. The full moon gave her enough light streaming through the window to see.

FRIDAY, AUGUST 1

During the night, I woke up with a horrible stomach ache. It was terrible, the worst I've ever had. Montezuma's Revenge, or something. I made my way into the bathroom and stayed for almost two hours. I missed Mom. She could help me feel better, she would know just what to do. Just her hand on the back of my neck would help, her soothing voice telling me that I was alright and I should go lie down in bed. My feet were so cold on the tile -- I was shivering for the longest time, then when I finally stopped freezing, I started to sweat, and I was too hot, burning up, and I couldn't get any fresh air! I wanted my Mama! Even my brother's curious eyes in the background would have been a welcome sight. I wanted my familiar room and our familiar bathroom with the pink, fluffy carpet and the dark pink towels hanging, having been carefully folded in thirds, all facing the same direction, and placed on racks around the room, one always within reach, and where was one now, when I really needed it? Where was that fresh smell of Downy on a towel that was never used more than twice before it was washed again?

I sort of drifted off and dreamed of home, but when I woke up, I was still in that cold, bare, blue bathroom, I still had a tummy ache and was feeling all clammy. I took a quick hot shower and finally felt a little better, well enough to go lie down for a while.

It was already past 8:00 by the time I got out of the bathroom! Lisa was still asleep. I whispered her name and she jumped up. I wasn't hungry. Lisa, for once, passed up a hot meal and just had a glass of milk and some cold cereal.

We got to school by 8:40, but the rest of our classmates were gone! They had gone downtown. Lisa wandered around el instituto while I slipped into a small room with a couch and took a nap. Lisa woke me up about an hour later and we went to Gregg's class, another boring hour of listening to notes on his future history book about Mexico. Why did he have to make it sound so DULL? This place is alive, and the history is all around us! He could have made it more exciting, but he must be accustomed to teaching from a stale classroom. He couldn't possibly make it fun and interesting, like this place is now! I can feel the spirit of all history of Mexico; this was a very hoppin' place, full of songs and laughter and people! But even the most fun time and place can be reduced to mere words on a page if it's not told right.

After class, Lisa, Diana, Linda and I got on the bus and went to Robinson. I told Dany I wasn't feeling well, and he told me he was off duty today. He told me he had come to the park just to see me, so we spent the rest of the day together, talking. He invited me to lunch, but I was too sick to eat.

Right now -- what time is it? I don't know -- I'm lying in bed, sick. I feel a little better than I did, but I'm still a long way from feeling good. I'm afraid to eat or move. I want to talk to Lisa. The house is completely quiet. I feel so alone. Why didn't Bart visit me? I went to see him when he was sick. I thought he was my friend. I don't want Dany to see me like this. I would love to see Bart now. Where is Lisa? No one to talk to, nobody cares about me. I miss Jeremy. I miss Mom and Dad. Maybe I can sleep through the whole weekend.

SATURDAY—SABADO, EL 2 DE AGOSTO
Yesterday, I slept most of the day. When I finally woke up in the early evening, I felt better and Lisa was here, she didn't desert me! She is a good friend.

Crystal was brought back to the present by the sounds of Sister Young praying in the living room. Could she have written the diary? Crystal silently put the diary in its hiding place, returned to her room and immediately fell asleep.

One night a couple of weeks later, Crystal had the chance to go again to read the diary. She wondered if the author was going to reveal her identity.

DOMINGO, EL 3 DE AGOSTO

I'm feeling great now, very happy! Muy feliz! Last night, Dany came and picked me up for another tour of the city! We drove all around the city and saw many more parks. We were out for about an hour. His beautiful eyes seemed to look into my soul, as if he could really see the real me. (No, I'm not in love. I'm NOT!) (Well, maybe just a little.) When he brought me home, it was still early. He kissed me softly and drove away.

I feel like I am learning so much Spanish! I know so much more than I did just a few weeks ago. I'm still shy, even though I KNOW no one will laugh at my mistakes. I must use Spanish while I'm here! This is the perfect chance. I will, I will!!

SUNDAY NIGHT, STILL AUGUST 3

Tonight I had a chance to practice Spanish with Cande and Miguel after dinner, mucho espanol! This was one of the few nights that Miguel was here for dinner, and I asked him why he isn't home much. He leaves for work at 4:30 a.m., six days a week, catches a train and rides for 3 hours to a milk pasteurizing plant, where he's a chemist. He spends 6 hours a day, 6 days a week, commuting! That leaves Cande to run the house by herself. She gets up at 3:30 a.m. every day so she can make his breakfast, then a friend of Miguel's picks him up and drives him to the train station.

I could never live in Cande's situation. For one thing, I need more sleep than she gets! She and Miguel never go out to dinner or dancing or to movies or anything! What a drag! Oh, well, they seem to be happy living like this. They certainly don't have much time for marital spats!

Lisa and I are getting closer. We are so much alike! I feel like I could talk to her about almost anything! I'm glad she's my roommate! Hasta luego!

LATER (STILL SUNDAY)

Ah, the metric differences! They buy gas by the liter here. Gas is priced by pesos per liter. These people never think of mileage, they think "kiloage."

I love my weight here. I only weigh 50! It's so neat! Bart weighs in the 80's. All those "Ideal Weight Charts" I have back home are totally useless here (until I convert them. But why convert? 50 is my ideal weight!)

When I was watching TV with Cande, we saw a guy who was dos metros, and another guy was dos-seis. Cande said they are both "muy alto." Two meters is about 6'6"!

One cultural difference that has nothing to do with the metric system is that Cande uses a frisbee to serve certain foods, likes chips and cheese. When I told her we use frisbees for sports, we throw them, she gave me this look of amazement, like, "using a serving dish as a sport?"

Oh, and the radio here isn't FM/AM, it's SW/BC.

Another difference is the bed sheets. They are made of the same material that flour sacks here are made of. They are light, yet warm, so without a blanket, I don't get cold.

That's the way it is, here in Mexico! So much for culture. What? It's 3 a.m.! Tres de la manana! Adios!

Again, Crystal heard Sister Young praying in the living room. Pastor Young had been gone for nearly two months and they hadn't heard anything from him. Crystal slipped down the steps. As she was about to enter the hall from the library, the phone rang. She glanced at the clock on the library wall and saw that it was nearly 6:00 in the morning. She must have fallen asleep again on the big pillow. She wondered who would be calling at this hour.

"Hello?" she heard Sister Young say. "Oh, hi, Rachel... no, you didn't wake me. I was just in prayer... What? Karen? On TV today? This morning? Okay, I'll turn it on now. I love you too. Talk to you later, bye."

Crystal followed Sister Young to the family room, staying out of sight. Sister Young turned on the TV, which hadn't been used in weeks, and found the National News Network.

Crystal curled up on the floor near one of the couches where she could see the TV but Sister Young couldn't see her. The TV volume was turned low.

Sister Young picked up the phone and dialed a number.

"Hi, Lisa," she said. "Are you watching NNN? Yes, Rachel called me and told me about Karen's story... Randall has been missing for a few months now, so the pastor left nearly two months ago to find him. We didn't really tell Rachel all the details about it because we didn't want her to worry, but I guess she and Karen did some. Rachel said that Karen could make anything known to the public... do you have it on? I think this is it." She kept the phone to her ear while she used the remote to turn up the volume on the TV. Karen's face filled the screen.

"We have just learned that two Americans, one a civilian and one in the Special Forces, have been taken hostage by rebels in a Central American jungle. The United States military has been denying this kidnapping for weeks, but our sources have revealed that these two men are being held for ransom. The rebels don't want money, but they want to keep the land they say is rightfully theirs, near this jungle at the bend of this river."

A grainy picture of Pastor Young and Randall in front of an old pickup truck filled the screen.

"The rebels have released this picture of the hostages, whom we have learned are Pastor Willie Young, and his foster son, Randall Derringer. Pastor Young is a civilian who lives near the small town of Goldendale, Washington. Derringer is in the Special Forces, and was stationed in Central America on a secret mission for nearly a year when he was taken hostage.

"According to our sources, the military refused to acknowledge that Derringer had been kidnapped, because they didn't want to compromise the confidentiality of their mission. Now that a civilian is involved, they have admitted that the original mission had been cancelled months ago, and the only thing still in progress had been a surveillance mission.

"In a National News Network exclusive, we will bring

you the stories of the wives of these two brave men, as we await a resolution to this horrible situation. I'm Karen Daly reporting."

Sister Young muted the television while she spoke on the phone. "Rachel mentioned that Karen is flying out here to interview us. Now that it's a national story, maybe it will help, somehow... can you come over with Karen? It would be really helpful to me... Yeah, I understand. Some people do have to work. Well, okay, keep in touch. I'll call you later, after the interview, to let you know how things go. Keep us in your prayers. Thank you, I appreciate that. Don't stop. I love you, too. Bye."

Crystal quietly slipped to her room before Sister Young noticed she was there.

CHAPTER 14

Rachel and the twins arrived at the farm that afternoon. Taylor and the boys were excited to see each other, and they had no idea of the real reason they had come. They ran down the path to the pond immediately after they arrived, while Crystal stayed inside the house, in the background, to hear and see what the grownups were planning to do.

"Karen is bringing her a camera crew here tomorrow to interview us," Rachel said. "It was funny, the other day I was talking to her on the phone about her new job, and she asked about Randall, and I told her that he was on some mission in Central America. While we were still on the phone, she was pulling up news stories from the wire and other places she gets news, and she found a short story that the military had released, a little story that seemed almost insignificant, about a military man, a secret mission and a civilian rescue effort and she guessed it was about Randall. So she made some calls and did some investigating, then she called me back and said she was really on to something. No one would say exactly what was going on, or who was involved, then she called someone else, acting like she knew all about it, and a secretary gave her a bunch of details, including Randall's name. Then, with that information, she was able to get a little more information from an Internet source, which eventually led to Dad's name, and the fact that Randall has been held hostage for quite some time, and that the military was trying to cover it up because they had made some major mistakes. They thought if they just said Randall had deserted, no one would know anything. They didn't figure Dad would show up and mess things up for them. So then Karen found out that Dad is also missing. We don't know if that is good or bad. So now Karen wants to interview us, to get the story in the news so maybe the government will do something about it."

"I'm not sure what good it will do for her to interview us," Sister Young said.

"She wants to get people interested in the story, to put

pressure on the government. If more people start asking questions, they are going to have to give some answers, or do something."

"I don't know about forcing the government to do anything, but I do know that if we continue to pray together, God can do something."

"We can pray that God will use the newscast to spread the word, so that something will happen," Rachel said.

"Let's just ask God to have His own way. He knows we have been faithful to Him, and He has always been faithful to us," Sister Young said.

"That's true," Rachel agreed.

The next morning, Kenny and Keith burst through the door, full of excitement.

"Mom! Mom! There's a TV news truck coming up the driveway! Grandma! A TV news truck is coming to your house!"

"We hear you, you don't have to shout," Rachel said, as Taylor came in the house.

"What are they doing here? Are we going to be famous?" Kenny asked.

"No, it's Karen. She is coming to ask me and your Grandmother a few questions," Rachel said.

"Is she going to make you stop eating sugar?" Keith asked.

"No, she wants to interview us," Rachel said.

"Is she going to make US stop eating sugar?" Kenny asked.

"No, she is just going to interview Grandma and me," Rachel said.

"Is THAT all?" Kenny asked.

"Oh, how dull," Keith said.

"Dullsville!"

"Duller than Dullsville!"

"SUPER-Dullsville, to the max!"

"Totally and completely!"

"Let's get out of here!"

"Beat you to the pond!"

"You can't beat me!"

"Can too!"

"Can not!"

"Can too! I can make it in 10 seconds flat!"

"Can not!"

"I can make it in five seconds flat!"

"I can make it in ONE second flat!" Kenny said, as they ran out the door.

For a change, Taylor stayed inside the house instead of going to play with the boys. She talked to Rachel and Sister Young. Crystal stayed out of sight when the news crew arrived, but close enough to hear what was being said. She slipped into the library where she would be able to hear everything without being seen. Karen knocked on the front door and Rachel invited her and the others to come in the house. Crystal peeked into the living room. One man had a huge video camera and another man was setting up lights and microphones in the living room. Rachel looked like she was going to start crying. Sister Young came in the room and greeted Karen.

When the camera and lights were all in place, Karen asked Rachel to sit on the couch so she could interview her. Then Karen looked out the window and decided to move everything out to the balcony. She said the background of the farm and the woods would make more of an impact on the audience, to see that the men being held hostage were not politicians or business people, but just ordinary folks who love their family and nature. Crystal couldn't hear what was being said on the balcony from the library, so she joined Taylor in the living room where they could both hear and see the interview without being in the way.

Karen asked Rachel and Sister Young, whom she called Claire, to sit on the deck chairs beside each other, so they could both be seen in the same shot, then the camera man could zoom in to each one when she was speaking. Karen stood in front of the camera with a microphone in her hand and began to speak.

"Rolling? Okay, three, two, one... I'm here at a remote farm outside of the small town of Goldendale, in Washington State, with the wives of two men who are being held hostage in Central America." Taylor shot a look of panic at Crystal, and Crystal thought about the fact that Taylor had no idea about what was really happening. All these weeks while Crystal had been listening to conversations, eavesdropping, actually, Taylor hadn't heard anything about it. Right now, Sister Young was too busy with the interview to notice that the girls were listening, and supposedly learning about this for the first time.

Karen continued speaking to the camera. "Rachel Derringer's husband, Randall, has been missing since the first of May. He was working on an undercover military mission when he disappeared, but the government has refused to assist him or even to admit that he has been taken hostage. They had unofficially labeled Derringer as a deserter. Rachel, did anybody in the military or government inform you that Randall was missing?"

"No, not at all. They haven't told me anything," Rachel said.

"Then how did you learn about this situation? How do you know what happened to your husband?" Karen asked.

"Randall has a twin brother, Vance," Rachel said, "who was stationed with Randall in Central America. Randall and another man were sent on a special assignment. Vance didn't hear from Randall for more than a week, then Randall's partner came back to the camp where Vance was and told him Randall had been taken hostage. Then Vance was transferred to the Middle East, and he came by here just before he went overseas. He told Pastor Young, who had raised him and Randall, what was happening with Randall. Pastor Young couldn't get any answers from the government, and he felt that God was leading him to go to rescue Randall, so he went. That was nearly two months ago. We haven't heard anything from him since he left, and we still can't get any answers from the government."

"After I was informed of this situation," Karen said, not mentioning the fact that Rachel was the one who had informed her or that she and Rachel were friends, "I did some investigating. At first, I got nothing but denials, then, finally, someone decided to speak up and tell the truth about what is happening with Sergeant Derringer and Pastor Young. Our sources have informed us that both are being held hostage by a rebel group who is fighting for their own land, which has recently been sold to developers, who plan to level the rain forest in that area and dig for oil. The developers refuse to budge on this matter, and they have no interest in saving the lives of these Americans either.

"Pastor Young's wife, Claire Young, is here with us this afternoon. Claire, what do you think about this whole situation? Do you think you will ever see your husband again?"

"I have no doubt, Karen," Sister Young said confidently, "because I know God is taking care of him."

"Do Randall and your husband speak Spanish?" Karen asked.

"No, neither of them know any Spanish," Sister Young said.

"Then how can they possibly communicate with their captors, who are known to hate Americans and speak no English?" Karen asked.

"I know God is able to do all things," Sister Young said, smiling, "and if I know my husband, he is taking this opportunity to preach the Gospel to everyone who will listen. Even if they don't know English, he will get the message across to them."

"Aren't you worried about your husband and Randall?" Karen asked.

"It won't do any good to worry," Sister Young said. "God has it already worked out. By faith, I believe I will see both of them walking through that door very soon, unharmed."

"Wow, you sure have more faith than I do," Karen commented.

"Faith is the substance of things hoped for, the evidence of things not seen," Sister Young said. "I believe it before it happens, and I am thanking God already."

"I don't know about all that," Karen said, turning to the camera, "but I do know these two ladies need a miracle to bring their husbands home. Would either of you like to add anything before we close?"

"I just want to ask everyone to pray for my husband and his dad," Rachel said, "to give them the strength to endure this ordeal, and please pray that they come home safely."

"Thank you, Mrs. Derringer and Mrs. Young," Karen said, turning to face the camera. We will continue to follow this situation as it develops. For National News Network, I'm Karen Daly. Three, two one, cut. How did it look, Marty?"

"Great, Karen, you were great," the camera operator said.

"Can you get some footage around here? That part will be aired as we taped it, but I want to do a follow-up story or two, until this gets resolved. Jeff, can you beam that story to headquarters?"

"Sure," the other man said, as he gathered the wires and equipment together.

"Oh, it's okay to get the boys on tape, if you see them playing outside, but please don't get the girls on camera," Rachel said. "They are kind of private."

"Sure, no problem," Marty answered, as he went outside with Jeff.

Crystal slipped away from the others and went to her room. A few minutes later, Taylor joined her.

"Crystal, did you hear what they were talking about?" Taylor said, visibly upset. Crystal stared blankly at the wall as Taylor moved about wildly in her peripheral vision. "Pastor Young and Randall were kidnapped! They are in real trouble! Crystal, I know you can hear me. Why aren't you upset? Don't you care about anything but your own stupid problem? Oh, I get it. You already knew, didn't you? You aren't even

131

surprised! You knew! Why didn't you tell me?"

Crystal didn't see any reason to break her silence now, so she just sat still, unresponsive.

"I can't believe it!" Taylor shouted, crying. "You are the most selfish person I know!" She went to the door, then turned back, "You're just like Daddy! You don't care about anyone else but yourself!" Taylor slammed the door as she left.

Taylor's words did not hurt Crystal, because she knew her sister was wrong. Crystal did not even care at all about her own self.

CHAPTER 15

A short time later, Sister Young came to Crystal's room with Taylor and they both sat on the bed beside Crystal.

"I can understand why you might be upset," Sister Young said. "We didn't want to tell you kids about all these problems, because we didn't want you to worry. I hope you heard what I said, though. We don't need to worry because we trust that God will work everything out. He will. Now that you know, I feel better, really, since I don't have to keep this secret from you any more. I just don't want you two to worry. What I do want you to do is continue to pray. Every time you think about Randall or Pastor Young, or even me or Rachel, please pray. We need to keep talking to God – not that we can change His mind about anything, but talking to Him will help us all feel better. He will give us comfort while we are waiting for Him to resolve this situation."

"When do you think they will come home?" Taylor asked.

"They will come home when God has accomplished His purpose," Sister Young said. "Everything happens for a reason, and nothing happens by accident. God is in control."

Crystal didn't know how Sister Young could possibly believe what she just said, but then, Sister Young didn't have to live with the problems Crystal had.

"Let's go in the family room and watch the news story on TV. Karen said it should be coming on soon," Sister Young said. Crystal followed the others to the family room and sat on one of the sofas. Karen and Rachel were drinking iced tea and talking and talking.

"Oh, here it is!" Karen said. Rachel turned up the volume with the remote control.

They watched the interview and Rachel laughed about how funny she looked. Seeing it on TV reduced it to a far-away news story, and didn't seem to Crystal like something that was happening to them, right now. After the interview ended, Karen stood up and announced that she had to leave.

Before she returned to New York, she was planning to go to Seattle and investigate a restaurant that was reported to be serving lizard meat. She and Rachel hugged each other and said goodbye. The camera operator and the other men were waiting in the van, and they left before the boys returned from their adventure at the pond.

After lunch, Crystal was planning to sneak upstairs to read more of the diary when she heard Rachel calling them to hurry into the family room. The twins were outside riding bikes, but Taylor and Crystal joined Rachel and Sister Young in front of the television. A senator was on the screen, talking about resolving the hostage situation in Central America.

"He's talking about helping us," Rachel said.

"I am committed, and I am asking for the help of not only the United States government in this matter, but also the government of Mexico and the Central American countries involved in this to help resolve this matter and bring our fellow American citizens home quickly and safely," the senator said.

"Thank you, Senator Bart Harper," the newscaster said.

"We don't want to prolong this situation any longer," Senator Harper said, "and I am willing to do whatever I can to help. I speak Spanish, and I have connections in that part of the world, so I am ready, if I am needed for negotiations. I don't want Claire and Rachel to suffer any more than they already have."

"That is really nice of him," Rachel said, when the news story ended. "Why would he go out on a limb like that, when everybody else seems to be afraid to even mention it? And that was weird, he called us by our first names. He must really be involved with this. Why would he do that?"

"Why indeed?" Sister Young asked. "Bart is just a thoughtful man, I suppose."

"Bart?" Rachel asked. "Do you know him?"

"No, not really," Sister Young said, smiling. "I wasn't even aware that he had become a senator."

Crystal looked at Sister Young. She wasn't acting like

herself; she seemed to be daydreaming or something, staring beyond the TV, with a peculiar look on her face.

"Well, I guess the important thing is that the story is getting national exposure," Rachel said.

"Yes, that is the important thing," Sister Young said distantly. "It's also important to plant good seeds, everywhere you go. You never know who God is going to elevate, and who He is going to use to accomplish a task. We are nothing but planters of seeds. The more good seeds we plant, the better the chances that good fruit will grow."

"Is that one of Dad's sermons?" Rachel asked. "Because it sure sounds like it."

"It's the truth," Sister Young said.

"Yeah, you're right," Rachel agreed. "You and Dad really planted some good seeds in Randall and Vance, and look how well they turned out. Really, all of your boys have turned out well. I'm surprised some of the others haven't been calling."

"They are so busy with their lives," Sister Young said, "I doubt that any of them are even watching the news."

"That's true," Rachel said. "But you know, so many people know Dad, I'm surprised the phone isn't ringing off the hook."

As if on cue, the phone rang. Sister Young motioned for Rachel to answer it.

"Hello? Yes... who's calling, please? Oh, hi! How are you doing? Good, good... yeah, I'm sure she wants to talk to you," Rachel said, handing the phone to Sister Young. "It's Lisa," she whispered.

"Hi! Yes, we did... wasn't that a good story? You must be really proud of her," Sister Young said. "Have you been watching that channel? Did you hear what our senator had to say?" She took the phone in the other room and Crystal couldn't hear what she was saying.

"That's Karen's mom, Lisa," Rachel explained to Taylor and Crystal. "She's a good friend of Claire's. They have known each other since high school, I think. I went to school with Karen, and so her mom and I are really good friends

135

too. Her mom is really cool. She's an artist, she paints and designs things and she is really good. Talk about planting good seeds, she really did a great job raising Karen. She was always an excellent student in school, so smart and motivated and outgoing. Look at her now! Not only is she famous, on TV every day, but she is going to help bring our boys back home."

Crystal thought Rachel was acting a little weird also, but she knew stress and worry about someone could make a person act in an unusual manner.

"I want to be a TV reporter when I grow up," Taylor said. Crystal was surprised to hear her say that. She had never mentioned anything about it before. Taylor wasn't nearly as shy as Crystal, and since she had broken her vow of silence, she may as well talk for a living, if that was what she wanted to do. She was pretty enough, with her black eyes and smooth black hair, but nobody would want to watch a mixed lady reporting the news on TV.

"You do?" Rachel asked. "Well, next time I talk to Karen, I'll mention it to her, and maybe she can give you some tips. She'll tell you what classes to take when you get in high school. You know, you can start by working on the school newspaper. Karen was so funny, she was like you, she always knew she was going to be a reporter. When we were in about the seventh grade, she had this tape recorder with a microphone, and she would make up questions to ask people, then record their answers. If she wanted to talk to the most popular girl in school, or a cute boy, she would just go up to them with her tape recorder and ask them how they felt about pollution or Santa Claus, or the math test they just took. And she always made the new kids feel welcome – she would interview each one. She asked them what school they came from, what was their favorite subject, if they liked sports or music. Then she made her own newspaper. Everybody read it and everybody loved it. Seventh graders couldn't work on the school paper – only 8th graders at our school – then when she was in 8th grade, she joined the official school newspaper.

She was the best reporter they had. Then in high school, she worked on the school paper and then while she was still in high school, she started her own TV news show, on the cable access channel in town. I helped her with it – I was her camera operator. I don't like to be in front of the camera. I prefer to stay behind the scenes. Karen used to always say I was the one who made her look good, but she really didn't need any help. She always looked good. I just made sure the picture looked good, you know, she was in the center of the frame and everything. She always had so much confidence. I learned a lot from her.

"Actually, I met Randall through Karen. She invited me to a picnic one day, with her family, and the Youngs were there with their kids, because, like I said, Karen's mom was friends with Claire. Karen had known Randall and Vance forever, so they were almost like brothers to her, and she introduced us. One of the twins kept staring at me – I couldn't tell them apart at first – and he sat by me when we ate lunch. I thought he was cute, but at first I liked the other one better, because he seemed so shy. I learned that the one who liked me was Randall, and he just kept after me. He told me that one day we were going to get married, and I just laughed. But then I got to know him, and a few years later, we did get married. You know, I think I loved him from the beginning, and he always tells everyone that it was love at first sight for him."

Sister Young came back into the room. "Well, are we going to fix some dinner?" she asked. Rachel followed her into the kitchen.

Taylor went outside to join the boys, and Crystal sneaked upstairs to read more of the diary. She was beginning to suspect that Sister Young really had written it. Crystal got settled on a big pillow and began to read.

JUEVES, EL SIETE DE AGOSTO
I feel like I've been bad, I haven't written in 3 days. I have been very busy, though (I know that's no excuse.) Tuesday we only had one class, our dance class, because Gregg and

Carlos were both sick. The one class we did have was very boring, so I'm glad it was the only one we had to endure that day.

Bart and I spent the afternoon in the park, just talking and relaxing. He hinted that he wants to get to know me better, but I quickly changed the subject. I like him a lot, but my heart belongs to Mr. Wonderful, Man of my Dreams, Dany. Bart is great as a friend, and I want to keep him as a friend, nothing more (and nothing less.)

"I know exactly where it is," Crystal heard Sister Young say, as she came into the library. "It should be right here on this shelf…" Crystal could hear her moving books around. "Hmmm, it was right here, with these others. I wonder if I left it upstairs?"

Crystal slipped the diary under the big pillow and tried to make herself invisible. She didn't want Sister Young to see her, or to know she had been coming here. She held her breath as she heard footsteps on the stairs, then they stopped.

"Oh, that's right, we were using it down in the pastor's office," Sister Young said, quickly going back down the steps. Crystal breathed a silent sigh of relief and slipped down the steps, out of the library and into her room as soon as they left the library.

After dinner, Rachel announced that she and the boys would be going home the next day, because they had an appointment in the afternoon that they couldn't miss.

"Are you going to be all right, here by yourself?" she asked Sister Young.

"Rachel, you know I'm not here by myself," Sister Young said with a smile. "I have the girls, we have the neighbors helping with the farm, and I always have Jesus, so I am never alone."

"I know, but we can come back if you need us," Rachel said.

"You just come back whenever you want," Sister Young said. "We love to have you here any time."

"Okay, maybe we'll come back next week. I have a few things to take care of at home."

"Our boys should be back home by then," Sister Young said.

"Do you think so?" Rachel asked hopefully.

"By faith," Sister Young said.

"By faith," Rachel repeated.

"Hey, why don't you guys come and visit us?" Kenny asked.

"We have the farm that needs care every day," Sister Young said.

"I mean, the kids, they could come."

"Maybe another time, Sweetheart," Sister Young said. "I need them to stay here and help me."

"Grandma! Don't call me Sweetheart!" Kenny protested. "I'm too big for that!"

"Excuse me, Honey," she teased.

"Honey! That's even worse!" he exclaimed.

The phone rang and Sister Young went to answer it. The boys ran outside while Taylor and Rachel went out on the deck. Crystal on her way to the library when Sister Young came through the living room with the phone and took it out to the deck.

"It's that guy from the government, Mr. Helmutt," she said, handing the phone to Rachel.

"Hello? Yes, this is she... no. No. I haven't heard anything. They what? Why doesn't somebody do something about it? Well, what about that senator who offered to help? We have to do something, somebody has to... what? You are saying an agreement is more important than two lives? No, I'm not going to calm down! This is my husband and my father-in-law we are talking about, not just anybody! They didn't ask for this! You can't just sacrifice them! You have to--" she stopped to listen for a long time, as she slid into one of the patio chairs.

"Thank you for calling," she said quietly, then she hung up the phone.

"So I take it he told you that they can't do anything," Sister Young said.

"He said their hands are tied, it's out of their hands, out of United States jurisdiction and all that," Rachel said. "He said they are withdrawing the troops from that area because it has become too dangerous, and they are just leaving Randall and Dad there. They are giving up because, they said, there is nothing they can do."

"Maybe they can't do anything, but God can," Sister Young reminded her. "From the time Randall first was taken hostage, the situation has been in God's hands. God saw the end from the beginning. He is not going to just leave them to die."

"But what about--" Rachel began.

"Ours is not to worry," Sister Young said. "Let's go to the altar right now." The two of them went to the altar in the living room and knelt together. Taylor joined them while Crystal sat on the couch, staring out the window. She had no doubt that they would be just as disappointed in God as she was. She heard Sister Young asking God to give them a sign, to comfort Rachel, and to help strengthen their faith. When they finished praying, they stood up, hugged each other, and walked out onto the deck. Crystal followed them.

"It really is a beautiful evening," Sister Young said.

"Yes, it is," Rachel quietly agreed.

"We have given the matter to God. Now let's just trust Him to work on it," Sister Young said.

"Hey! Look at that rainbow over there!" Taylor shouted, pointing toward the mountain.

"Look! It's complete, end to end," Sister Young said. "Rachel, you know we don't believe in a pot of gold at the end, but what do we believe about rainbows?"

"It's a reminder that God always keeps His promises," Rachel said.

"Didn't we just ask God for a sign?" Sister Young asked.

"Yeah! That's a sign from God!" Taylor said excitedly.

"God really is working on it," Rachel said.

140

"Yes, He is," Sister Young said. "So let's just let Him work, and trust Him to take care of our boys."

Later that evening, they were all watching television when a news report came on announcing that the United States was unable to help in the hostage situation, and they were pulling the troops out of the area.

"Karen's story has been picked up by the big boys," Rachel said. "Now it is really well known. I just wish someone could help."

"Rachel, you don't need to make a wish," Sister Young said. "Didn't we put our trust in God?"

"Yes, sorry, it just slipped out," Rachel said.

"God answers prayers, He doesn't grant wishes," Sister Young said. Crystal disagreed with that statement, because God didn't answer her prayers.

"Grandma, could we have some popcorn?" Kenny asked.

"Yeah, popcorn!" Keith said. "Popcorn and a movie!"

"Please?" Kenny asked.

"Well, because you said 'please,' I guess we can have some," Sister Young said. "Why don't you boys come and help me make it?"

"I can put the bag in the microwave," Kenny offered.

"We don't have a microwave," Sister Young said.

"Then how do you make popcorn?" Keith asked.

"We have a popcorn popper," Sister Young said.

"The old-fashioned kind? Cool!" Kenny said.

"We'll help you!" Keith said, as the twins and Taylor went to the kitchen with Sister Young.

Rachel began to change the channels to look for a movie when she came across another news story about the hostage situation. She turned up the volume. The speaker was very handsome, with light brown hair and blue eyes, and was identified as Daniel Vasquez, the president of Mexico. He was speaking in Spanish. His words were translated into English, printed at the bottom of the screen.

"I will do everything I can to help to resolve the United

States hostage situation in Central America," Crystal read. "Perhaps the United States government can't do any more to help, but I have friends in that part of the world. I am going to speak to them."

The interviewer asked President Vasquez why he was getting involved.

"It is my duty as a leader to do all I can to help, and it is my duty as a Christian to help other Christians. One of these men is a pastor, a missionary. He's not a military man. These men have nothing to do with the struggle going on in Central America. They should not be held any longer. I don't want the families of these men to suffer any more than they already have." The printed words stopped as he said in English, "I am going to do what I can to bring these men home to their wives and families in the United States."

"That was the President of Mexico, President Daniel Vasquez, offering to do what he can to resolve the hostage situation in Central America," the reporter said, then he went on to the next story. Rachel turned down the volume.

"That's strange," Rachel remarked. "Why would the President of Mexico get involved in this situation?" Crystal wondered the same thing.

Taylor and Kenny and Keith brought popcorn in several bowls and set them on the table. Sister Young brought a tray with glasses of lemonade for everyone.

"Claire, we just saw the strangest thing on TV," Rachel said. "There was a news report that showed the president of Mexico, and he said he is going to help to resolve the hostage situation."

"Praise God!" Sister Young said. "God answers prayers."

"Yes, but don't you think it's odd," Rachel asked, "that the president of Mexico would be concerned about two American men who are being held hostage?"

"God works in mysterious ways," Sister Young said. "If the president of Mexico is the person God is using, I say, let's praise God."

"Until just now, I didn't even know who the president of

Mexico was," Rachel admitted. "I didn't even know they had a president. But now I know I will never forget his name."

"What is his name?" Sister Young asked, handing a glass of lemonade to Crystal.

"Daniel Vasquez," Rachel said. "I didn't know Daniel was a Mexican name."

"Daniel Vasquez is the president of Mexico?" Sister Young asked, with a strange look on her face.

"Yes, have you heard of him?" Rachel asked.

"What did he look like?" Sister Young asked, suddenly very interested.

"He is really handsome, kind of young looking," Rachel said.

"Did he have blue eyes?" Sister Young asked.

"I think so, why?" Rachel asked.

"I think he was once in the Olympics," Sister Young said.

"What movie are we going to watch?" Kenny asked impatiently.

"Let's watch the one on the Family Channel," Sister Young said, changing the channel and changing the subject.

Crystal knew now that the diary was true. Dany was the same Daniel who was now the president of Mexico, she was sure of it... and that senator's name was Bart, the same Bart from the diary. Lisa, the writer's roommate, was Karen's mother. That meant Sister Young had to be the author of the diary, even though she looked much younger than 47. It was all true, it had all really happened. Crystal was curious to read the rest of it to find out how it ended. She wondered why Sister Young hadn't married Dany. However, she couldn't go read now because she didn't want anyone to know she had been reading it, and if she were to get up and leave the room, she would be noticed. She sat in the room with the others as they watched the movie, but she didn't pay any attention to it. She was thinking, trying to remember what the diary had said about Bart and Dany, so she could compare them to the two important men who had just announced that they were responding to the crisis that was affecting someone they knew; only neither of them mentioned that they knew Sister Young. They must have seen Karen's interview on TV and recognized her.

"Earth to Crystal," Kenny said, bringing her back to her current surroundings. "Hello, are you in there?" She blinked and looked at him blankly.

"I asked if you want some popcorn, if you're not too spaced out in your own silent world," he said.

"Kenny, leave her alone," Rachel said. "Don't bother her."

"If we don't talk to her, she's never going to talk to us," Kenny said.

"Yeah, she'll never be normal if we just let her dissolve into the background," Keith said.

"All she has to do is just start talking," Kenny said. "Then she'll be normal, like Taylor."

"It's a lot more complicated than that," Rachel said.

"Complicated?" Kenny said. "If we stopped talking, you would just tell us to cut it out and to answer when we were spoken to."

"You could never stop talking," Keith said.

"Neither could you," Kenny said.

"Could too."

"Could not."

"Could too!"

"Could not!"

"Boys! The movie is starting again," Rachel said. "Crystal doesn't have to eat any popcorn if she doesn't want any."

"I was just asking if she wanted some," Kenny said.

"Shhh!" Keith said. "This would be a great time for you to stop talking, right now, so we can hear what they are saying in the movie!"

"YOU stop!" Kenny said.

"I DID stop!" Keith said.

Crystal looked at Taylor, the twins, their mother and Sister Young, and thought about how pointless it would be for her to start talking. She had nothing to say to these people. She didn't want to be with them right now; she didn't want to interact with them in any way. She didn't need them and they certainly didn't need her.

CHAPTER 16

When the movie ended, Taylor followed Crystal to their room.

"Aren't you ever going to talk again?" Taylor asked. "Not even to me?"

Crystal sat on the bed without responding.

"I don't want you to be like this," Taylor said. "I just want you to get back to normal. The twins are right. You just need to start talking and then you will be normal again."

Crystal didn't feel normal. She didn't feel anything at all. She didn't need to talk any more. She didn't need people bothering her or intruding into her private life, her thoughts, her emotions. She thought about that song that Daddy had on a tape, about being a rock or an island that didn't feel any pain or cry. She was like that now, not attached to anybody. The pain was gone, even the emptiness was gone. She was just a shell on this earth, with no life inside of it.

"Everyone around here is always saying that God does everything for a reason," Taylor said. "I think He brought us here for a reason. He gave us everything we need here. We have a lot more than we had in Tennessee. Look at this big house, and the animals, and the woods and the pond, and this family that loves us more than Tammy and her family did. Look at all the brown people here. They want us here. They don't make us feel different. They bought us all those clothes and stuff, and they said we can decorate our room however we want. We have all the food we want here. Don't you remember how hungry we were back home?"

Crystal still didn't answer. Her life in Tennessee was like a fading dream. The details Taylor mentioned were unimportant now. She didn't remember. Even the recurring nightmares had stopped. The only thing from Tennessee she was still holding was her guilt over Daddy's death. The rest was so far away from her now. Even the fond memories of Daddy were hard to recall, they were so far back down at the end of that long, dark tunnel.

"Well, even if you don't remember," Taylor went on, "I do. Our life here is so much better than it was there. Just forget about all that and be thankful for what we have here."

Crystal realized that Taylor was starting to sound like the Jesus freaks around here. She wasn't like herself any more. She was always happy and bouncing and cheerful. She was completely disrespectful to the fact that their father was dead.

"Let it go, Crystal," Taylor said. "Grow up."

Crystal knew that Taylor was just trying to trick her into saying something. Her ploy didn't work. Crystal would not be provoked to argument like the twins often were. She did not need to explain, she did not need to communicate. Nothing inside of her needed to be exposed to anyone, not even to Taylor. There was nothing inside of her at all any more.

Taylor turned out the light and got in bed. Crystal waited until she heard her breathing heavily, then checked the hall to be sure everyone else was asleep. She didn't hear any sounds or see any lights, so she quietly slipped into the library and up the stairs to return to the diary. In the bright moonlight, she began to read.

VIERNES, EL OCHO DE AGOSTO
Today was the big history test, which wasn't too hard, but not that easy either. Gregg came up with all kinds of questions that we didn't cover in class. I guess he used information from all those lectures we attended, and all those churches that Lisa and I didn't attend. I passed the test, I suppose. I correctly answered most of the questions. Until yesterday, I didn't expect to take any tests on this trip. I sort of forgot we were going to school here!

After we finished the test, Lisa and I walked next door to get some ice cream at a tiny ice cream shop. The shop is unlike any in the states: very dark inside, with flies flying all over the place. All they sell is ice cream, no sundaes, no milkshakes, and they have the strangest flavors, with chunks of fruit in them. The boy who works there speaks no English, but he let us taste some different flavors to see if we liked them or not. None of the flavors were like the ones we know, chocolate, vanilla, chocolate chip mint. They were all very unusual. I tasted one that was papaya, with chunks of strawberry, another was mango flavor with bits of oranges, and there was a type of apple flavor with apple chunks and cinnamon in it. I selected lime, which was white with pieces of real lime in it. It was great! I'm not sure what Lisa had, something pink with several kinds of fruits and nuts in it. I didn't like that kind, but it was interesting.

SATURDAY—EL SABADO, EL 9 DE AGOSTO, 6:10 P.M.

Wow, I still don't believe this. This isn't real. I am in Mexico? Can't be, no way. Me? Never. But it's true! Too strange to describe, it must be felt. I feel great!

Today we decided to go swimming at Robinson. Bart and Diego just happened to be on the same bus as we were, but they were really snotty to us. Did we care? No. I don't know what their problem was, but we didn't let it bother us.

Dany called me over to talk to him when we first arrived, and I got those chills/thrills like I always get when I am with him. I stayed with him most of the time we were there, but I did watch Bart dive off the top platform. (I thought he was going to chicken out and climb back down the ladder, but he went for it! He was braver than I thought he was! He looked pretty good, too. I was almost impressed!) Manuel told me he hurt his toe yesterday. Pobrecito!

Lisa told me it was time to go, then Dany asked me to kiss him, right in public! I think he wanted to see what Bart's reaction would be, because Bart was watching me most of the afternoon, but I didn't care what Bart saw or didn't see. (He didn't see us kiss.) No me importa! Then Dany asked me to find a date for Manuel tonight, we are going to double date! All right!

SUNDAY MORNING, AUGUST 10, 8:10 A.M.

More unreality, but I'll just tell the story. It all seems too strange to be true. Dany was right on time, but he was alone. Lisa agreed to go with us Where was Manuel?

Downtown . Fine Let's go get him. Fine. Dany was acting very strangely, but I couldn't put my finger on what his problem was.

When we turned onto Coronado, the car died, so I had to drive for half a block while Dany push-started it. Lisa thought that was the most hysterical thing (since the last time we got into hysterics) and she couldn't stop snickering. We drove around the city, circling the downtown area. Where was Manuel? No answer. On to the gas station, where I had to keep my foot on the brake while Dany filled the gas tank, so the car wouldn't roll into the street. The car died again, so Dany pushed again. Time to find Manuel. Where was he? Dany was driving all over the place, seemingly at random. He stopped the car and got out for a minute, then he got back in, with no explanation. The car died again. He asked me to push this time. No problem! (He laughed.) When he turned the key, it broke off in the ignition, a good reason for Lisa to panic in her moody, near-hysterical state. I didn't believe that the key could break so easily, but when Dany lit a match to examine it, I saw the key, broken in his hand, and I felt the other part stuck in the ignition. Now what ? How could the car go? Dany matched up the two pieces and turned the key, a task that I didn't think was possible. I began to laugh hysterically with Lisa.

When Dany got the car going again, we suddenly found ourselves behind a bus. Dany told us that Manuel was coming on the bus. No way did we believe him. Too coincidental! Dany whistled loudly out the window. The whistle was repeated from outside. I looked all around for Manuel, but didn't see him.

"A finger!" Lisa exclaimed, pointing at the back window of the bus. All I saw was a fingernail, then a finger. A moment later, black hair. He materialized like the Cheshire cat, one portion at a time, finger, smile, hair, face, and it was Manuel! We followed the bus for about two blocks and when it stopped, Manuel stepped off the bus and Dany let him into the back seat with Lisa. Dany acted as if this were all normal, and Lisa and I exchanged glances, silently acknowledging that we don't know what's normal in Mexico!

We drove around until we were near the same place Dany took me on our first date. We piled out of the car and turned on the radio, at top volume. We danced, out in the country, in the fields. Dany and I slow danced while Manuel and Lisa did the bump. (Apparently, the bump is very popular here, but I had never heard of it before I came to Mexico.) We danced so close to each other, we almost seemed to be one person. Dany whispered in my ear that he loved me, and he held me very close. I had almost forgotten that we weren't alone when Lisa told me she needed me to go with her on a nature walk. At first, I didn't understand what she meant. Wasn't it a too dark to see any nature? Then I realized that she meant the call of nature, and I felt it also.

Away from the guys and the light of the car, it was very dark, and I kept tripping over sagebrush. Lisa was babbling about something that made me giggle. Then she stopped and I bumped into her.

"Did you hear that?"

"What?"

Silence.

"What?" I repeated.

I thought she was trying to scare me, but then I heard it. Los lobos! Wolves! They sounded as if they were far away, but if some were far away, maybe some were close also. Yikes ! We did what we had to do and attempted to run back to the car. I fell over something and then leaped and bounded to where the others were waiting. No problem! No, I'm not afraid, no tengo miedo de NADA! (Good thing I didn't think about SNAKES!)

Dany and I walked a short distance from the car. He put a leather ankle bracelet on my right ankle and told me he'll never forget me. Over the music, Lisa's voice drifted to my ears.

Suddenly I felt like it was urgent for us to return to the car. Neither of us could see very well in the total darkness, so we followed the sound of the music. When we found the car, Lisa was saying she needed to go. I thought that she meant home, but she meant that she had to go for another nature walk. We didn't want to get too far away from the safety of the car, in case the wolves decided to get closer. (I don't mean the guys, I mean los lobos.)

"Before we return to the car," Lisa whispered, "I need to figure out something. What is going on? Why is everything so unusual to us, but they act like it's so normal?"

"Like what?"

"The key broke off in the ignition. Dany wasn't even worried about it, like that happens all the time, but I would be extremely nervous if that ever happened in my car. When I mentioned it to Manuel, he shrugged it off as if it were not important at all, the most usual thing in the world."

"I know! But things are so different here."

"And what about Manuel and the bus? A finger, an eye? How did Dany just happen to be behind the right bus at that time? There were about 50 buses downtown, and at least 4 on the same street at that time."

"That did seem rather odd."

"Rather odd? It was eerie! And the way they whistled to each other. How could we hear it all the way from the bus, and how could Manuel have heard it?"

"That must be their code whistle or something."

"Well, do they always have to push the car? I'd sell my car if I had to push it so many times! And who is going to push it from here? We are on flat land, in a field! I hope the battery doesn't die with the radio on all this time!"

"Stop worrying, they know what they're doing." I hoped my voice had more confidence than I did, but to be honest, I wasn't one bit worried over the possibility of us being stranded out in the desert with these two wonderful guys.

When we finally did return to the car, the guys told us they had been worried about us.

"We thought you were lost!" Dany said.

"Los lobos didn't get you!" Manuel added. No, they didn't.

Lisa and Manuel went for a walk and Dany sang me a love song in Spanish. I closed my eyes for a few minutes while he sang to me.

When I opened my eyes, Dany's mood was suddenly different. He had become distant, not smiling. Was he upset with me? He looked at me with a very serious expression on his face.

"What? Que? Please tell me what's the matter!" I begged.

"We can't go out any more," he said flatly, looking away from me.

"Why not? I'll be here for about another week..." I began.

"No. I have a girlfriend. A Mexican girl that I am going to marry next year."

He didn't have to say any more. I had been used. That explained so many things. Why hadn't I seen it coming? Why had I let myself fall in love with him? I felt that my final humiliation would have been to let him see me cry, to admit to him that when he had told me he loved me, I had believed him. I felt like I had to pretend that I had been using him also.

"No me importa, I have a novio also," I told him.

He moved closer to kiss me, but I had to turn away from him. I couldn't bear to kiss those lips and know they were reserved for someone else. My thoughts were so painful, but I didn't want to feel; I started to feel numb. His words kept ringing in my head, 'No. I have a girlfriend.' I didn't hear another word he said. I wanted to get away from him as soon as possible.

Lisa and Manuel returned and we were home before I realized what was happening. (I don't know if they had to push start the car or not. My mind had left the scene earlier.) Dany kissed me goodnight and seemed confused when I refused to return his kiss. I followed Lisa into the house and didn't look back at the car. I never want to see Dany again!

Lisa asked me a couple of questions, but I pretended that I was too tired to talk. I didn't have the courage to confess to her that my heart had just been broken, that my world had been crushed, that I had been used by a beautiful, seductive man. I felt so stupid. I went straight to bed.

I feel a little better this morning and when Lisa wakes up, maybe I'll tell her what happened. Maybe we will celebrate my freedom from love, my freedom to be myself without the face of a man in my mind at all times. I feel like crying now, so I can't write any more.

Crystal had intended to finish reading the diary, but she fell asleep after reading those few pages. The sun was rising when she awakened. She hid the diary and went down the steps.

As Crystal stepped into the hall, Sister Young was coming out of her room.

"Crystal," she said quietly, jumping slightly. "You scared me. I didn't think anyone else was up yet. Are you all right?" When Crystal didn't respond in any manner, Sister Young said, "Come with me to the altar to pray." She took her hand softly and led her to the altar. They both knelt.

"Dear Father in heaven," Sister Young began, "we come to You this morning, thanking You for another day. Thank You for waking us in our right minds, and thank You for Your many blessings. You are great, You are good to us, You are loving and kind. You care for us, and You take care of us. Father, we come to You this morning asking that You guide us this day in everything we think, do and say. We ask that You forgive our sins, as we forgive those who have sinned against us. We ask that You give traveling mercies to Rachel and her boys as they travel today. Father, we ask that You bless my husband and Randall, that You touch them and comfort them, that in every situation they would keep their minds on You. Father, we pray for the ones who are holding them hostage, that You would touch their hearts to let them go. Father, we ask that You bless each person who has come forward and offered to help with this situation. We ask that You give us peace in this matter, and in every matter. Only You can solve our problems. We look to You, our Provider, our Comforter, our Hope. Father, we leave our burdens with You, knowing that only You are able to take care of everything. Touch Crystal right now, and her sister too. We praise You, Father, and thank You in advance for what You are going to do. In Jesus' name we pray, amen."

Sister Young stood and began thanking God and clapping her hands. Crystal also stood, and when she saw that Sister Young was clapping and thanking God over and over, Crystal went to her room and got in her bed. Taylor was still asleep, still breathing heavily. Crystal began to wonder if God might be listening, if He might have a plan in mind. Everything seemed to be too much of a coincidence; maybe He did have a plan. Maybe He would bring Pastor Young and Randall home safely, and maybe what had happened in Mexico thirty years ago was part of His plan. Crystal could almost see the situation like a big puzzle, with the pieces being put in place to make it complete. She just didn't see where she fit in this puzzle, or why she was here. She remembered something that someone had said recently, that God sees the bigger picture and all the people in the world only see a tiny portion of that picture. She thought about how insignificant she must be to God, with all the other important things that were happening in the world. She almost could forgive Him for not helping her, when she realized how small she was in His plan for the whole world. She wondered if maybe He was just too busy to take care of her; not that it mattered, because she didn't really need anything from Him, or from anyone else any more.

CHAPTER 17

By the time Crystal awakened later that day, Rachel and her boys had already left. Taylor and Sister Young were outside with the animals. Crystal saw cereal and a place setting for her on the table, but she decided to go for a walk instead of eating. Sister Young had told her to get some fresh air and exercise every day, so Crystal was just being obedient.

She began to walk on the trail around the property, then she took the path to the Top End and the overlook of the Back 40. She stood by the rock where she and Rachel had sat together and looked down at the fairy tale land. She could see the deer trail from the other side of the valley, going to the pond. She stood there, staring, until the whole scene began to look like a giant patchwork quilt, carefully constructed. She thought about how it must look from the air, this portion connected to the rest of the property, and how they fit into the bigger picture of all the farms and woods in this area, and realized that only God could have put all of this together to make it fit so perfectly. She pictured a globe in her mind, and thought about how all the pieces were put into place by God. She realized that He put things together in space, and He put events together in time. He did have a plan, it was so clear to her now, even though she still had no idea where she fit into it.

That evening, Sister Young and Taylor asked Crystal to walk with them to the pond. She followed them as they chatted about the pets and the wildflowers and the frogs. She became aware of the sounds the frogs were making, and thought about how God was also a symphony conductor, putting each croak together, transforming them from ugly frog throat sounds into a musical masterpiece. They stopped and looked at the pond, which Sister Young said was considerably low for this time of year, then they walked across the property to the cabins. Sister Young said that in the fall, they usually housed a family or two who needed a place to stay. She opened the doors and looked into each cabin while Crystal and Taylor walked around the garden and the play areas for the children.

They walked back to the house, arriving while it was still light outside. Sister Young asked them if they wanted to watch a movie on TV or read a book, and Taylor said she would like to see if she could find a good book to read. Crystal followed her to the library but didn't feel like looking for a book. She sat in one of the comfortable chairs and stared out the window as the landscape changed from color to black and gray, as the evening grew dark. She thought she could hear Sister Young turn on the TV, and she wondered if she were watching the news. They hadn't heard anything since last night's news, but Sister Young was so confident that God was answering their prayers and that everything would be fine. Crystal thought about going upstairs to finish reading the diary, but she decided against it, since she didn't want Taylor to know anything about it.

Later, after Taylor had gone to bed and fallen asleep, Crystal again sneaked up the steps to finish the diary. The moon wasn't shining tonight, so she couldn't read without turning on a light. She decided against it, because it was too risky. She didn't want to get caught reading the diary. She slipped back down the steps and went back to bed. For a while she couldn't sleep, then the picture of the landscape quilt filled her mind. As she again wondered how she fit into the picture, the pieces of the quilt seemed to rearrange themselves, then fit together perfectly in another way. As she was falling into sleep, the thought that God could solve problems another way, a different way, His way, slightly comforted her. She fell into a deep, dreamless sleep.

CHAPTER 18

Two more weeks passed without any word about Pastor Young and Randall. The phone was ringing often. Sometimes reporters were calling, and sometimes friends and family were calling, but nobody had any news. Sister Young spent her nights praying and her days with Crystal and Taylor. She encouraged them to help her in the kitchen, with cooking and cleaning, in the gardens, and with the animals. They took walks together every morning and often again in the evening when it wasn't too hot. Sister Young spoke to Crystal but didn't press her to talk. She suggested that Crystal respond in some way, with a nod or a movement. A few times, Crystal thought she might reply, but she just didn't feel right. After months of not saying anything, nothing seemed important enough to say.

With all the walking and activity every day, Crystal was falling asleep quickly at night and couldn't stay awake to read the diary. She was busy all the time and didn't have any time to herself during the day or evening. She wanted to finish reading the diary. Finally, one evening she forced herself to stay awake until she heard Sister Young go into her bedroom. At last, Crystal had an opportunity to return to her hiding place and the diary.

MARTES, EL 12 DE AGOSTO
Hello again! On Sunday, Bart called right after I woke up and asked me to go to a movie with him. Of course! Bart, thank you for saving my life! What better way to get one guy out of my mind than to see another guy?

LATER, THE SAME DAY
Bart invited me to go to see a movie tonight, so we went. I couldn't concentrate. I didn't understand it at all. After the movie, we walked around downtown for awhile and I bought some gifts for my family. Bart didn't buy anything, but he informed me that last night everyone from the school had a birthday party for him - everyone except me was invited.

Man! They all kept it secret from me! Why didn't they want me there? Who organized it? Do I really care? (Yes.)

I was wondering why Bart wanted to take me out tonight, out of the blue. He was so emotionless, as he usually is, I couldn't tell how he was feeling. Am I being too sensitive? I like Bart a lot. I feel (a little bit) jealous that I wasn't invited to his birthday party. I still feel let down by Dany, betrayed, hurt. Must be on a downward swing... well, I guess it's not that important. Who cares about some stupid party anyway? I'm really sleepy now. Goodnight.

Crystal stopped reading. She suddenly felt guilty: she felt like she was intruding into Sister Young's private life. She didn't want to read any more of her diary. She was about to close the book when several folded papers fell out of the back of the book and onto the floor. Crystal unfolded the papers and saw they were in the same handwriting.

SATURDAY, AUGUST 23 – HOME FROM MEXICO!
Man! I can't believe it. Oh, man! Right when I got home, Mom asked me if I had a good time and if I was okay. I said yes, and before I could tell her anything about my trip, she told me she had bad news for me. The look on her face said it was really bad, and I wondered if someone in our family had died. Well, I was right - someone did die, but not someone in our family. Mike killed himself, right after I left for Mexico. Mom didn't have any way to contact me; well, I guess she could have figured out a way, but she probably didn't want to ruin my trip, so she didn't try to send me a message or anything. That would have ruined my whole summer, the whole experience, if I had known. There I was, clear in another country, enjoying myself, carefree, going on with my life (while he should have been going on with his) not really even thinking of him, and he went and killed himself! Does everything really happen for a reason? What is the reason behind this?

SUNDAY, AUGUST 24

Talk about not believing it! Mike's mom called today, when she found out I was home from Mexico, and she said it was all my fault! If I hadn't just left him, she said, he would be alive today. She said he left a suicide note that said he was doing it because of me! Why did I break up with him? I mean, I know why I did, we just weren't right for each other and he was so jealous and so possessive, but if I had just let him think we were going to be together when I got home, he would be alive today. It was all my fault! I could have saved his life! I was so selfish! All I could think about was my freedom, the trip, and my life away from home. Why did God let this happen?

Crystal knew exactly how she felt. She eagerly turned to the next entry.

MONDAY, AUGUST 25

Can a person who kills himself go to heaven? I heard that he can't, because he can't ask for forgiveness, unless there is a moment, or even just an instant, between the time when he commits the act, before he dies, that he asks God to forgive him. So... if he is in forever in hell, then it is my fault.

TUESDAY, AUGUST 27

School is starting Tuesday, and I don't want to go. Everyone will be blaming me. Everyone else in the whole school, just about, was at his funeral, except me. I don't want to see anyone! I wish I could be invisible! What a complete downer. Why do I have to go to school, for this, my senior year? Maybe Mom will let me transfer to another school. She has to understand! She tried to tell me it wasn't my fault, but because of me, because of what I told him before I left, he is not alive today! How could it not be my fault? Everyone is going to hate me. What a killer girlfriend I turned out to be.

WEDNESDAY, AUGUST 28

Mom and Dad could tell I was really having problems with this whole suicide deal, so they took me to see Pastor Friday. At first, I didn't want to say anything to him; I never wanted to talk to anyone, ever again. What could I say? How could I even ask for forgiveness, for something I didn't mean to do? Or, I meant to do it, I meant to break up with him, but I never thought about what might be the consequences of my actions. How could I have known? But Pastor Friday was so nice and so understanding. He wasn't blaming me. I was afraid when Mom and Dad left the room that Pastor Friday would really let me have it... and he did. He let me have the Word of God. He read a couple of scriptures to me, and they were comforting. Romans 8:38-39 assured me that nothing can separate me from the love of God. Pastor Friday gave me a list of Psalms to read every day, and as we read some of them together, I began to feel better already.

Then Pastor Friday told me that it wasn't my fault. I don't know how he knew what I was thinking, if Mom and Dad told him, or if God told him. But Pastor Friday so kindly said, "It wasn't your fault at all. You didn't give him the gun. You didn't pull the trigger. You didn't force him to do it. It was completely his own decision. We are each responsible for our own actions. You are not responsible for his actions." I wish he would tell Mike's mom that. Even though Mike said it was my fault in his letter, it _wasn't_ my fault. I didn't do it. How typical of him, to blame me for something he did, and then make me feel guilty, like it was my fault.

It wasn't my fault!

I asked him about Mike's fate or his final place of residence, and Pastor Friday answered my question about where he is... what a relief! I was way off in my assumption. Pastor Friday made it so clear to me. He first reminded me that Jesus died for all of our sins, past, present and future. He died for all of our sins before we were even born, before we had committed any sins. When He died for our sins, almost 2000 years ago, ALL of our sins were our future sins.

He died <u>then</u> for the sins He knew we were going to commit after we were born: all of them. So as long as a person has accepted Jesus Christ as his or her personal Savior, all of that person's sins are forgiven, including future sins that haven't been committed yet. Mike and I had talked about church and Jesus a few times, and he told me he had accepted Christ when he lived in Seattle, when he was 14, before we met. So, because of his faith in God and his acceptance of Jesus, he is in heaven now! It was his choice to accept Jesus, and it was also his choice to take his own life. I am so glad Mom and Dad took me to see our pastor.

It wasn't my fault! Whew!!!

THURSDAY, AUGUST 29

It might not be easy, but I am ready to start school with a guilt-free conscience. I am expecting some people to blame me, but I know for sure it was not my fault. Maybe everyone will be so wrapped up in themselves and their own summer vacations, they won't take the time to pick on me. Maybe by now they have forgotten what happened almost three months ago.

TUESDAY, SEPTEMBER 3

I was wrong! As I often do, I projected a gloomy future (kind of like the weatherman does) and then I was so relieved when it didn't come true (like the bad weather forecasts.) Today at school, everything was great. Everyone was so sympathetic and nobody blamed me. A few people said they felt sorry for me. I didn't want that kind of attention, but at least I was able to go to school without feeling guilty. I even saw Mike's brother, and he said he knew it wasn't my fault. He asked me to forgive his mom — and I already did — because she was just so upset, she had to take it out on someone. She does not know Jesus, so she has no Comforter. We prayed for her.

Now, to go on with my life, which I think has taken a turn for the best, and leave those things behind which are behind me. I will never forget about my trip to Mexico, but that was just a part of my life and now I will go ahead, upward and onward, to whatever God has for me! Thank God for working everything out for me – like He always does! What will my senior year hold in store for me (besides an advanced Spanish class)? And what better things does God have for me?

That was the end of the writing. Crystal held onto the loose pages tightly as she began to absorb the meaning. She felt a flood of emotion wash over her.

"It wasn't your fault at all...You didn't force him to do it... It was completely his own decision... You are not responsible for his actions... It wasn't my fault... It wasn't my fault... It wasn't my fault."

The words on the page spoke to Crystal, as if they had been written just for her to read. Maybe Daddy's suicide was *not* her fault. She hadn't given him the gun. She hadn't pulled the trigger. She hadn't told him to do it. She couldn't even think of anything she had done to make him mad at her. She couldn't have known to go to him even one minute earlier to stop him from what he was planning to do. Nobody had ever told her that they blamed her. She had only blamed herself.

She thought about individual responsibility. Daddy had made his own choice. Daddy had also made sure she and Taylor understood what it meant to accept Jesus as their personal Savior. Daddy confessed that he knew Jesus too... Jesus died for all of Daddy's sins, including his final sin for which he may not have had a chance to ask forgiveness... so he must in heaven right now. If Daddy was not suffering now, why should she continue to suffer? Taylor had been right. This was time for Crystal to live, not to merely exist.

Suddenly, she felt very tired; not tired in her body, but tired emotionally, tired of being pushed down, farther and farther by the guilt and pain she had piled on top of herself. She couldn't sink any deeper or she would be completely crushed. She had to let go of the burdens she had been carrying all these months. She had become so attached to her burdens, lugging them around with her had become her lifestyle. She tried to imagine what it would be like to be free... what she could do, how she would live if she were to let them go. She could envision a rainbow beyond her cloud of blackness. The time had come for her to get out from under it all, but she knew she couldn't do it alone. She thought about Jesus and she felt like she was reaching for His outstretched hand.

She noticed she was crying. Tears were running down her face. She began to feel an emotional release. She was feeling again! Hurt, shame, guilt, sorrow; then turning into comfort as she let go of them. She realized she was kneeling. She spoke to God without speaking aloud and she let Him have all those painful feelings while she accepted His comfort. She felt His warm touch, first on her head, then down her shoulders, through her back, all the way to her feet.

Crystal thought she was crying aloud; yet the sound of the crying was coming from downstairs, from the living room. She could hear Sister Young crying out to God, crying for her husband's safety, for her son's safety. She was telling God that she trusted Him to take care of everything, and she was asking Him to strengthen her faith.

Before she knew what she was doing, Crystal had made her way down the steps and into the living room. Sister Young was kneeling at the altar, bent all the way over, with her face almost touching the floor. Crystal's heart was pounding, aching, feeling once again, as she gently put her hand on Sister Young's shoulder. Sister Young was thanking God for what He was going to do. She was thanking Him for bringing her husband and son home safely. She reached up and touched Crystal's hand.

When she saw that it was Crystal who was touching her, she began crying with a smile on her face.

"Crystal! Thank you! God knew I needed your touch," Sister Young whispered. "Oh, did I wake you? I must have been getting sort of loud."

"No, I was already awake, Crystal said. "I need to tell you something."

"Are you all right?" Sister Young asked.

"I am so sorry," Crystal apologized.

"You don't need to be sorry, for anything," Sister Young said gently. "I am so glad you are here right now. And you are speaking! Is anything the matter?"

"I'm okay. I'm starting to feel better."

"Hallelujah!" Sister Young shouted, giving her a hug.

"Is Pastor Young coming home?"

"I am trusting that God will answer my prayer. I believe He already has, and He will soon confirm it!"

"I hope so."

"He will," Sister Young said with confidence. "He is working it out already."

"Have you heard anything?" Crystal asked.

"Nobody has called me and I haven't seen anything on the news lately," Sister Young said, "but I know God is working on it. I know He has a plan and He is doing it His way."

"But what about when His plan is different from our plan?" Crystal asked.

"His plan is almost always different from ours, but we have to accept it. His plan is greater than ours, because He sees the big picture and we can only see a small portion of it."

"But what if His plan is..." Crystal began, "what if a person has to die?"

"When a person dies, and that person knows Jesus, we should rejoice for that person, because he is with Jesus forever. We mourn for ourselves, because of the void in our lives, but that person who is with Jesus would not want to come back to be with us if he had the choice. And Jesus has promised to comfort us, the ones who love Him. Even though sometimes we would like God to answer our prayers a specific way, we really need to always be praying for God's will to be done."

"You were asking God to bring them back home."

"God says in His Word for us to ask and we shall receive, so I have been asking, and I am expecting to receive."

"But it has been so long since you have heard anything," Crystal said.

"God is working in His own time," Sister Young said. "We can't lose faith and we can't forget His promises, just because He isn't moving as fast as we would like. In the Bible, some people had to wait years for their prayers to be answered, or for God to fulfill His promises. We can't get discouraged when God doesn't move right when we expect Him to move, or if He does something in a different way than we are expecting Him to do it. We just have to keep trusting Him, and believing His Word."

"Even if He doesn't answer our prayers?" Crystal asked.

"God always answers our prayers, but sometimes His answer is not the answer we want," Sister Young said. "Sometimes He says 'yes,' sometimes He says 'no,' and sometimes He says 'wait.' But He always answers prayers."

Crystal thought about her prayers that she thought God hadn't answered; then she understood that He *had* answered them, but He hadn't given her the answer that she had wanted. She had assumed that because He hadn't done what she had asked, He hadn't answered at all. She had been shutting Him out because He hadn't done what she wanted Him to do. She felt now that His comfort had always been available to her, and she just hadn't accepted it.

Crystal looked up at Sister Young, who no longer seemed like a stranger to her, but now she saw her as a complete person, a girl who had been hurt and survived, who had friends in high places who still cared about her, even if she wasn't in contact with them any more. Crystal was curious about the diary, about the writer of the diary, the person she had been and the person she was now.

"I found a book," Crystal began, then she started to cry.

"What book?" Sister Young asked kindly.

"I didn't mean to be snooping around, I just found it..."

"We don't have any secrets here. You are welcome to read any book you find in this house."

Crystal opened her mouth and then closed it again. She couldn't tell her about the diary. All this time she had been reading it as if it were just a book, but now she was standing next to the author. The character in the book had come to life. She looked at Sister Young and saw a different person, knowing she had been the young woman in the diary. Crystal realized now that she knew some of Sister Young's secrets and innermost thoughts from her past, and although they were healing words to Crystal, she could not confess to Sister Young that she had read her diary, that she had invaded her privacy. She suddenly felt like an intruder into a life that had been lived long ago, a trespasser in a personal journey.

Crystal stood and silently cried while Sister Young wrapped her arms around her. They stood there for a long time, just hugging. Now that Crystal was beginning to feel again, to feel the love Sister Young was giving her, she didn't want to make her mad at her. She wanted – no, she *needed* to receive the love that was being given to her and she could not hinder the flow by telling her that she had read her diary.

"Crystal," Sister Young said softly, trying to comfort her, "everything is going to be all right. Let me know what you need and I'll do whatever I can to help you."

Right now, all Crystal needed was to be held and loved. "You already are," she said.

Taylor came padding into the living room. "What's going on?" she asked. "I thought I heard voices."

"Crystal and I were just having a talk," Sister Young said.

"Crystal was talking?" Taylor asked, astonished.

"Yes, I was," Crystal answered, drying her eyes with her hands.

"Whoa!" Taylor said. "I thought you were never going to talk again."

"I guess, for a long time, I didn't need to talk to anyone," Crystal said, shrugging, "and then I just needed to talk to Sister Young, so I did."

"Just like that?" Taylor asked.

"Just like that," Sister Young said, snapping her fingers.

"Well, it's about time," Taylor said. "Wait 'til Kenny and Keith hear you talk," Taylor said. "They thought you had a serious problem, and they thought you were really weird. I tried to tell them you were okay, but they didn't believe me, they just judged you by what they saw. But now that you are talking, they can't talk about you not talking anymore. You are going to keep talking, aren't you?"

"Yeah," Crystal said. "I don't really have a reason not to."

"So you're finally letting it all go?" Taylor asked.

"I gave it all to God," Crystal answered. "I let it all go."

"That was a very wise decision," Sister Young said.

"Speaking of Kenny and Keith, when are they coming back?" Taylor asked.

"I'm not sure," Sister Young said. "They are taking swimming lessons this month. Now, aren't you girls sleepy? It's almost 3 a.m. Let's go back to bed."

Crystal led the way to the bedroom, with Taylor following close behind her.

"So what made you start talking?" Taylor asked, after she got in bed and turned out the light.

"I guess I was just finished with not talking," Crystal said. She wanted to tell Taylor about the diary, but she didn't want her to know she had been invading Sister Young's privacy. She began to relax and felt like she could easily fall asleep.

"I saw something on the news about Pastor Young and Randall," Taylor said.

"You did?" Crystal asked, immediately wide awake. "What was it?"

"Well, they didn't mention their names, but a news reporter – not Karen, but some man – said that the president of Mexico or someone had completed some negotiations and the hostages should be released soon."

"When did you hear that?" Crystal asked. "Did you tell Sister Young?"

"I was just going through the channels after dinner, when she was cleaning up the kitchen."

"So did you tell her about it?"

"No, I forgot."

"You forgot? How could you forget?"

"I found a movie I wanted to watch, and I just forgot about it until now," Taylor said.

"I'm sure she wants to know," Crystal said. "She has been praying and praying about this."

"Should we tell her now?" Taylor asked.

"No, let's wait until morning," Crystal said. She thought about Dany, the president of Mexico, whom she felt like she knew personally, or at least, she knew him when he was younger. She wanted to watch Sister Young's reaction carefully when Taylor mentioned his name. How odd it must be for a person, a boy she had loved so long ago, to come back into her life this way, to save her husband's life. Now Crystal was wide awake, thinking about the diary, the life that had been lived, and tried to make it transform into the life that Sister Young was living now. What had happened in her life, between then and now? As she connected the two lives together, she began to see Sister Young as a young woman, not much older than herself, who was just living in an older person's body. Then she thought that really, Sister Young wasn't that old; she was just in her 40's, which wasn't really ancient, like some of her teachers in Tennessee, who had been in their 60's. Maybe Crystal had something to look forward to in her life. Maybe she did have a reason for living, a reason that God would reveal to her later, when the time was right. Maybe God had brought her here to find and read the diary, so she could be healed; and be loved.

The next morning at breakfast, Crystal reminded Taylor to tell Sister Young about the news report she had seen last night.

"Sister Young, I forgot to tell you, I saw something on the news last night about Pastor Young," Taylor said. "The guy on the news – not Karen, but some man – said that the president of Mexico has negotiated the release of the prisoners, I mean, hostages, in Central America. He didn't say Pastor Young's name, but that's who he was talking about."

"Praise the LORD!" Sister Young shouted. "Thank God! Thank God! Thank You, Lord, for answering our prayers!

I'm sure we will be hearing something soon."

She called Rachel and told her the good news. Rachel said she would check with Karen to see if she had heard anything more about their situation or when they would be released, and she would call back as soon as she discovered anything.

CHAPTER 19

The phone did not ring all for the next three weeks. Crystal, Taylor and Sister Young settled into a routine of taking care of the gardens and the animals, and going to the chapel on Sundays. Very few people were coming to church, but Sister Young said it was always that way in the summer, when people were either really busy with their farms or on vacation. The Sunday services were a prayer and testimony time, with people taking turns reading scriptures. After Sister Young shared the good news that Pastor Young and Randall had reportedly been released, the neighbors were constantly asking if they had called or if she had heard from Pastor Young. Sister Young didn't have anything more to tell them, except that she was believing God would bring him home soon. Crystal wanted to believe that was true, but her doubts were growing with each passing day. She wondered if Sister Young had any doubts.

Near the end of summer, Rachel called and said Karen would be doing another report on TV in the evening about the hostage situation. Crystal and Taylor sat beside Sister Young on the sofa while they waited for the report. Taylor fidgeted impatiently while Sister Young silently prayed.

"I think this is it," Crystal said, as Karen appeared on the screen.

"Nearly four months have passed since an American pastor, Pastor Young, disappeared in a Central American jungle while attempting to rescue his foster son, Sergeant Randall Derringer, who had been taken hostage earlier by local rebels. After Senator Bart Harper offered to help and then American authorities refused to get involved, Mexican president, Daniel Vasquez, stepped in to assist. He negotiated the release of the two hostages nearly a month ago. However, since the date of their alleged release, nobody has heard from the hostages nor from the rebels. An undercover international task team has infiltrated the hidden rebel camp, only to find that it has been abandoned, with no trace of Pastor Young or Sergeant Derringer.

"This time, authorities are speaking, only to say that the prognosis is not looking good for Pastor Young and Sergeant Derringer. Notes found at the abandoned site indicate that the plans of the rebels were to kill the hostages, then commit mass suicide. A task force is now searching the jungle for the location of the suspected murder/suicide, in an attempt to stop this atrocity before it happens.

"For National News Network, I'm Karen Daly reporting."

"Did she say that Pastor Young and Randall are going to be killed?" Taylor asked, with a look of worry on her face.

"She might have said that, but I don't believe it's true," Sister Young said. "God has the final say about what will happen, and His report is the only one I believe."

Crystal wanted to tell her not to be so optimistic, because bad things do happen when they are least expected. She thought Sister Young was being very unrealistic; Crystal knew from her own experience. Since Sister Young was so positive in her belief, her faith was so strong, Crystal decided not to say anything to upset her.

The next day at church, all the neighbors came to give their support to Sister Young. The church was more full than it had been all summer. Everyone Crystal had met, plus many other people she hadn't seen before, were there. Many were crying and expressing their grief over the situation. Some had brought dishes of food and sympathy cards.

Deacon Eagle stood at the podium and began to speak, slowly and deliberately.

"We want to thank everyone for coming today, and we thank God for this family, and the man of God, our pastor, and how he sacrificed his life for his son. We all knew Pastor Young, we all loved Pastor Young and his son, Randall. Sister Young, we all want to let you know that we are here for you, and if there's anything you need, anything we can do for you--"

Sister Young stood up and stopped Deacon Eagle in the middle of his sentence. She turned and addressed the congregation.

"Good morning," she began, "I appreciate all of you and the support you are showing in this situation, but Pastor Young is still alive."

The congregation gasped.

"Where is your faith?" Sister Young asked. "Pastor Young and Randall are not dead. We have been praying, all of you have prayed with me for both of them. Where is your faith? Do you all believe man's evil, gloomy report? Or, in this case, woman's gloomy report? Don't you believe our God can deliver them? Don't you believe He will answer our prayers?

"I believe He is answering our prayers already. I believe He has already released them from their captors. I believe Pastor Young and Randall are on their way home right now. This is not a funeral or a memorial service or a wake! This is a time for us to rejoice, and believe that God is doing for us what we have been asking Him to do."

The church members were silent. They looked at Sister Young with unbelief, until Mother Brown stood up and began clapping her hands.

"Praise God, for what He has done," she shouted, still clapping. "Faith is the substance of things hoped for, the evidence of things not seen. We should thank Him in advance for what He is going to do. Isn't He good, all the time?"

"Amen!" several people shouted.

"So let's act like He's good!" Papa Brown added. "He hasn't brought us this far to leave us! Whose report do you believe? Man's? Or God's?"

"God's!" everyone shouted.

The whole service turned into a praise service, with person after person testifying to the goodness of God and everyone singing and praising God. By the time the service had ended, Crystal had begun to feel like Sister Young was right, that God was going to answer her prayers and bring Pastor Young back home.

Sister Young announced that after service everybody was welcome to stay and eat; the food which had been brought would be served at a potluck. The whole mood had been transformed from mourning to rejoicing, and all the neighbors stayed and enjoyed the food and the fellowship.

That evening, Rachel and her boys arrived. At first, they were upset over the news report, but Sister Young gave them the same words of encouragement she had given the neighbors that morning in church. Rachel began to feel better, and the boys were thrilled when Sister Young insisted that their father and grandfather were still alive. Crystal still had a nagging doubt, but she didn't want to put a damper on things, so she didn't mention it.

"Hey, it's neat that you can talk now," Keith told her.

"Yeah, you're not so weird any more," Kenny said.

"Yeah, you're just like normal now," Keith said.

"Yeah, like a normal person," Kenny added.

"Thanks," Crystal said.

"You are welcome," Kenny said.

"You are a well cone," Keith said.

"You're welconian, you Draconian," Kenny said.

"You're a Draconian," Keith said.

"You are!" Kenny shouted.

"Not that again!" Taylor said, and they all laughed.

CHAPTER 20

All week, Crystal enjoyed the company of the twins, as she and Taylor explored every corner of the property with them. The boys weren't as interested in the Back 40 as she was; they preferred to play in the woods and at the pond. They picked ripe peaches and pears off the trees and ate them; they also picked not-so-ripe sour apples and ate them too. Crystal didn't even mind being around the animals. The kids helped harvest some of the fruits and vegetables and they all enjoyed going in the hot tub in the evenings and up to the library tower to look at the stars at night. Crystal was beginning to live again, and to enjoy her new life.

Crystal didn't think any more about the diary; she was thinking about life now. She had to continually force herself not to think about what might be happening to Pastor Young and Randall. She wanted to believe they would be home soon, like Sister Young kept saying, but in the back of her mind, she didn't expect things to work out the way they were hoping they would.

One hot afternoon Crystal and Taylor were playing in the woods with Keith and Kenny, where it was shady and cool. Keith was climbing a tree, trying to tie a rope onto a thick branch so they could hang a tire swing from it.

"Hey, a truck is coming up the road!" Keith shouted from his perch in the tree.

"I think I hear it!" Kenny said.

"Who is it?" Taylor asked, since the twins seemed to know everybody in the area and which vehicles they drove.

"I don't know, I haven't seen that one before," Keith said, trying to get a better look. "It's turning into our driveway!"

"Let's go see who it is!" Kenny said, as Keith scrambled down the tree.

The four of them ran through the woods to the house, just as a new blue truck stopped by the garage. Three men were in the truck.

"It's Dad!" Kenny yelled.

"Dad! Dad! Grandpa!" both boys shouted.

Pastor Young and Randall got out of the truck and the boys ran to hug them. Crystal almost couldn't believe her eyes. They were dirty and thin, and their clothes were ragged, but they were alive and they were home.

"There's no place like home," Randall said, hugging both boys at the same time.

"You can say that again," Pastor Young said, joining the hugging. "Come and give us a hug, girls. You don't know how happy I am to see you! Group hug!"

"What is all this commotion – praise God!" Sister Young shouted, as she and Rachel came out of the house. They ran to greet their husbands. The entire group hugged for several minutes.

"Thank God," Rachel said, crying. "Thank God."

"Are you okay?" Sister Young asked.

"Yes, we are, by the grace of God," Pastor Young said.

"What happened? We didn't hear anything on the news about you being back in the United States," Rachel said.

"It's a long story. Oh, meet Manuel, he gave us a ride all the way from Mexico City," Pastor Young said. "Manuel, come on in the house with us."

Manuel got out of the truck and they all went in the house.

"Do you want some water, lemonade, iced tea?" Sister Young asked.

"I want some lemonade!" Kenny shouted, jumping up and down.

"Me too!" Keith said.

"Water for me," Pastor Young said.

"Water sounds great," Randall said.

"Yes, water, please," Manuel said.

Crystal and Taylor helped Sister Young with the drinks, while Rachel attached herself to Randall.

"Have a seat, relax," Rachel said, as they all gathered around the dining room table, "and tell us all about what happened."

"Dad came and got me," Randall said. "Then we came home."

"That's the condensed version," Pastor Young explained.

"Does the military know you're here?" Rachel asked. "How did you get away from the rebels? Did they feed you? Why didn't you call? Why wasn't anything on the news? The last we heard, you were about to be killed and nobody could find you."

"Did you have to fight them?" Keith asked, punching the air.

"Yeah, did you give them a karate chop?" Kenny asked, demonstrating.

"Calm down, boys, and let your father and grandfather tell the story," Sister Young said.

"Can we get something to eat first?" Pastor Young said. "Maybe get cleaned up, change our clothes, stretch our legs? Then we can tell you all about it."

"Do you want me to call Karen?" Rachel asked. "She would love to get exclusive news coverage on this story, especially since it has a happy ending."

"Karen, your friend Karen?" Randall asked.

"Oh, I forgot, you don't know," Rachel said. "Karen got a job as a reporter for National News Network, and she had been covering your story, ever since Dad disappeared. Dad, were you kidnapped too?"

"Later; we'll tell you all about it later," Pastor Young said, standing and stretching. "Manuel, let me show you where you can take a shower."

"I'll show him," Sister Young said, "while you get your shower."

"Me too," Randall said.

"It's a good thing you have three bathrooms with showers in this house!" Kenny remarked.

"Thank God! He always provides what we need," Pastor Young said.

The house was a buzz of excitement all afternoon. Rachel and Sister Young prepared a celebration feast, with Crystal and Taylor helping. The boys were so happy to see their father, they couldn't stay still. Everyone was so thankful that the ordeal finally had ended.

After the men had changed into clean clothes and everyone finished eating, they all moved into the family room to hear the story.

"Why don't you start, Randall, then I'll add to it," Pastor Young said.

"I guess the beginning is the best place to start," Randall said. "Well, I was just doing my duty, standing guard one night, way back in April, with another guy, Morton. We were at our camp, and nothing unusual had been happening. We weren't on any alert or anything, we were just there. We weren't really on a secret mission or anything, we were just watching for any type of unusual activity. I'm not really sure why they even sent us down there. So anyway, Vance was with us, but he had day duty, I had night duty. This one night, I thought I heard something in the jungle behind me, so I turned around, then I felt something metal hit my head, like a shovel or something. I saw stars, then everything went black. When I woke up the next day, Morton and I were chained to this old abandoned pyramid thing, somewhere in the jungle, and these guys were sitting across from us.

"We were there a few days, they fed us a little, but not much. I guess they didn't want us to die. They were trying to use us as bargaining tools. They only spoke Spanish around us, and my Spanish isn't that great, so I didn't really know what they were saying, but Morton sometimes knew what they were saying. Then one night Morton escaped, he got away during the night. After that, they chained me even tighter, and kept a closer watch on me. The days all ran together, and I don't really know how long I was there. I was just there, sleeping and kind of waking up and sleeping some more. I think they were giving me some kind of drugs in my food, or the food was making me sleep, or something.

"Anyway, one day Dad showed up. I thought I was dreaming or hallucinating. He was kind of hidden in the jungle. I didn't know if I really was seeing him or not. Then one night, they weren't watching me and Dad came over to me and unlocked the chains and we just walked away."

Pastor Young began to tell his part of the story. "I found a guide to take me part of the way down the river, on a boat, but he wouldn't go all the way with me because he said it was too dangerous. Just before we got to the end of our journey, where he was going to drop me off, the boat capsized, and I had to swim to shore. I saw the guide swimming to the other shore, and he just made it before an alligator or crocodile got him. I lost everything I had, except what I was wearing, when the boat sank, including my passport. I had a little bit of money in my pocket, but it couldn't do me any good in the jungle. I started walking. I just kept praying and asking the Lord to lead me, step by step. God directed me right to the site where they were holding Randall. I stayed out of sight for three days and three nights, and then when the rebels left Randall alone one night, I went over to him and unlocked the chains and set him free."

"How did you unlock the chains?" Kenny asked.

"They had left the keys with a bunch of other stuff in one of the tents," Pastor Young said.

"What did you eat?" Keith asked.

"God always provided food for me," Pastor Young said. "There were these little banana trees all over the place, with small bananas, so we ate a lot of those.

"Can we have some popcorn?" Kenny asked.

"We just ate dinner," Rachel said.

"But it's like we're watching a movie when Grandpa tells the story, only we watch it in our head," Kenny said.

"Just listen, and let them finish telling it," Rachel said.

"Anyway, they were getting ready to abandon the place before I even arrived," Pastor Young said. "Apparently they were planning to just leave Randall to die there – but God had another plan. They also left some food behind, so we took what we could with us. We walked back the way I had come, for two or three days, going very quietly..."

"And we were always watching for snakes," Randall added. "There were lots of snakes in the jungle."

"Eeewww!" Taylor said.

"We came around one corner," Randall said, "and we were following a trail, and this huge snake – maybe a boa, I'm not sure – was just hanging from this tree. We almost ran right into it, and it pulled back like it was going to spring right on me—"

"And I just spoke to it," Pastor Young said, "I said, 'In the name of Jesus, I claim the authority over you!' and the snake recoiled back into the tree and left us alone. We just walked right by it."

"So we kept walking for a couple more days, all the way back to the military camp," Randall said, "and that had also been abandoned, so we got some more food from there, and we just kept walking for a few more days."

"Didn't you sleep?" Kenny asked.

"We stopped every once in awhile," Pastor Young said, "when we found a good hiding place, under a bush, in a little cave, once we even climbed a tree and slept up there. We tried to take turns, so one of us would be awake and watching, but sometimes we both were so exhausted, we both fell asleep and God watched out for us. Really, He took care of us the whole way."

"We kept walking and walking," Randall said, "and we didn't really know the way to go. God guided us. I didn't have my passport either, and we somehow crossed the border of two countries, by going through the jungles."

"One day we came upon a tribe in the jungle," Pastor Young said, "and God gave us favor with them. They fixed us a huge feast and tried to get us to stay with them. A couple of the men knew a little bit of English, and they were all so nice to us."

"Of course, Dad preached to them," Randall said.

"Of course," Sister Young said, smiling and nodding knowingly.

"And they were receptive to the Gospel," Pastor Young said. "One guy translated what we were saying, and some of them accepted Christ, and we ended up baptizing seven men under a waterfall. It was the most beautiful sight. We stayed there with them for a couple of days so we could rest and recharge."

"Then we started walking again," Randall said. "We weren't even sure what country we were in, but God was leading us, and we just kept going. He gave us the strength, even when our food ran out and we couldn't find any more little bananas."

"Oh, yes, the desert," Pastor Young said. "We had a huge desert to cross. We walked all night and we slept in the shade of a tree or a rock or a cactus during the day when it was so, so, so hot. But God provided water. He led us from a watering hole to a tiny waterfall in a little rock formation to an oasis where there was a pond and a bunch of trees, and then we kept walking until we came to water."

"Water!" Randall said. "It was the ocean, we think, and so we just started walking north on the beach, which we figured was toward the United States. We still didn't know what country we were in."

"And neither of us had our ID or our passports," Pastor Young added. "We got a ride on a sail boat to somewhere – we weren't even sure, because the sailors all spoke some other language."

"I think it was Portuguese, because it wasn't Spanish," Randall said. "So they took us to this one port, it must have been in Mexico, and they said something to a guy on the docks, and the guy – he spoke English – said he would give us a ride to Mexico City. He had this old farm truck with only one seat inside, and a wooden bed in the back that was filled with hay. He told us to get in, and you have no idea how comfortable that bed of hay looked to me! So we climbed in and we rode for three or four days with him, and he took us to some government buildings. We were thanking him and asking how we could repay him, and he just asked us to pray for his wife, who was about to have a baby. So we were wondering what to do, which direction to go, then Manuel showed up and we started talking, and he offered to drive us all the way home. We tried to explain how far it was, but he just kept grinning and saying he would drive us home. We told him we didn't have our passports, and he said he had the paperwork we needed. He got us across the border, I don't know how. We rode with him for six or seven days, until we finally got home."

"Does the military know you are here?" Rachel asked. "I don't want them to think you are AWOL."

"As far as they are concerned, I am dead," Randall said. "We saw some paperwork at the camp. I wanted to bring it, but Dad said to just leave it there. I don't even exist any more."

"We're going to straighten them out," Pastor Young said, "as soon as we get a little rest."

"Tell us more about your adventure!" Kenny said.

"Yeah, like, how did you keep walking when you were so tired?" Keith asked.

"The joy of the Lord is my strength," Pastor Young said.

"Did you have to fight the rebels?" Kenny asked. "Pow! Pow! Pow!" he shouted, punching the air.

"No, like we said, God just sent Dad to release me, and the rebels were already gone," Randall said.

"But didn't you fight them before that?" Kenny asked, sounding disappointed.

"No, I didn't have a chance," Randall said. "Weren't you listening to what I said? They hit me from behind. I didn't see them coming."

"I would have just flipped them over and then done a back flip over them," Kenny said.

"Yeah, and then I would have karate chopped them," Keith added.

"I'm sure you would have," Rachel said, then to Randall, "so, can I call Karen, so she can let the country know that you have made it home safely? Everyone has been so worried about you, especially the neighbors and church members, but thank God for Claire. She has been a rock of faith. She hasn't wavered or doubted that you would be coming home. She has been constantly reminding us that you were in God's hands and that He was answering our prayer. We just had to wait on Him and believe it."

"God answers prayers," Sister Young said.

"You better believe it," Randall agreed.

"Amen!" Pastor Young and the twins shouted together.

Crystal noticed that Manuel had fallen asleep in the recliner. Sister Young looked in his direction, then indicated to Pastor Young to look at him.

"He could sleep downstairs, or we could let him just stay here, on one of the sofas," Sister Young said. Pastor Young went over to him and nudged him, suggesting that he stretch out on a sofa. Manual just rolled over onto his side in the chair and began snoring.

"He has driven the whole way, all the way from Mexico City," Pastor Young said, "and he has only had a couple of hours sleep in the last few days."

"Let's go in the other room and let him sleep," Sister Young suggested.

"I have a better idea," Pastor Young said. "I think I will follow Manuel's lead and go to bed too."

"Me too," said Randall. "I can't remember the last time I slept in a bed, but it must've been at least six months ago."

"Let's go up to the tower balcony and watch the moon come up," Kenny said.

The men went to bed and the rest of the family climbed the steps to the tower, just as the sun was setting. Crystal looked out over the landscape with its changing colors and was amazed by the beauty of the whole area. She felt a surge of relief come over her, as if she could now breathe again, after holding her breath for months. She felt a sense of peace, and she knew God was touching her with His peace right at that moment. She closed her eyes and silently thanked Him.

"Hey, look over there!" Keith shouted, interrupting her state of tranquility. "Who is that?" Crystal saw three vans coming up the driveway. As they got closer to the house, she could see that they had some kind of logo on the sides.

"It's Karen!" Rachel exclaimed. "I just called her a little while ago. How did she get here so fast, I wonder?"

Rachel lead the group down the stairs and out to the driveway near the garage, where the three vans were parking.

"Rachel!" Karen said, "Let's get this show on the air! We are ready to go live as soon as you are."

"How did you get here so fast?" Rachel asked.

"I was already in Portland when you called, and I had the trucks standing by and ready to go," Karen said. "I was planning to come out here tomorrow anyway and do a follow-up interview, to get the story hot again, but you've got a better story! Hey, Steve, Marty, can you set up in the house? Boys, can you show these men to the living room, where they can set up the equipment?"

"Sure," Keith said.

"Hey, want to see the man who drove them all the way home from Mexico City?" Kenny asked. "He's asleep, but you can still look at him." The twins took the camera crew into the house.

Crystal looked around and noticed Manuel's truck wasn't there.

"Where did his truck go?" Crystal asked.

"That's right," Rachel said, "it was parked right here." They looked around the parking area, but the truck was no longer there.

"Maybe it's inside the garage," Karen said.

"No, our cars are in the garage," Sister Young said.

"He's gone!" Kenny shouted, bursting through the door, with Keith close behind. "He just disappeared!"

"You know what he is," Taylor said. "He is an angel."

"How can he be an angel?" Kenny asked.

"No, really," Taylor said, "God just used him to bring back Pastor Young and your dad, and then he disappeared with his truck."

"Can angels eat?" Keith asked. "Because he ate with us."

"Did you actually *see* him eat?" Taylor asked.

"Well, no," Keith said. "Did you, Kenny?"

"Ummm, I don't remember," Kenny said.

"So, no one really saw him eating," Taylor said. "He's an angel."

"Well, I can tell you, he IS an angel," Rachel said, "to me. He brought back the two men I love most in this world."

"Hey!" Kenny yelled. "What about us?"

"She said men, not boys," Taylor said.

"Although this is an unusual twist to the story," Karen said, "maybe I just better stick with the facts."

"Randall and Dad are already asleep," Rachel said.

"Well, that's okay," Karen said, "I'll just interview you and Claire, and then we'll do another live feed in the morning, or whenever they wake up. I want the world to know that your nightmare is finally over and they are home."

They all went inside the house, and this time Crystal watched everything closely. She was interested in what the men were doing with the cameras and the lights and microphones, and she wondered if she might work with cameras some day. She and Taylor sat on the sofa while Karen interviewed Rachel and Claire. Almost as if on cue, Pastor Young came into the living room wearing his bathrobe over his pajamas, and Karen began asking him questions. He repeated the story he and Randall had told earlier. Just as he was finishing telling what had happened, Randall came out looking for his wife, and Karen interviewed him also. Kenny and Keith were in the family room watching the interviews live on TV.

When Karen had signed off her report, after encouraging her audience with the happy ending to this harrowing experience, Kenny reported to the family that the interview on TV was about two seconds behind the real life interview.

"It was really weird, because we could hear everything twice, like an echo," Keith said.

"Do you know why that is?" Karen asked. "It's because we were beaming the interview up to the satellite, and then it had to come all the way back down to earth to our news station, and then they sent it back up to the satellite to be beamed back down to all the news stations who were carrying it. So that's quite a distance to go in such a short time, don't you think? All the way to outer space and back, twice?"

"Wow!" the twins said together.

"Did you interview Manuel?" Randall asked.

"He left," Rachel said.

"He left?" Pastor Young said.

"He disappeared," Taylor said. "He was an angel. God just sent him to bring you guys back home."

Pastor Young and Randall exchanged glances.

"Speaking of going quite a distance in a short time," Randall said under his breath.

"Karen, do you and your crew want to stay the night?" Sister Young asked. "We have plenty of room for everyone."

"No, thank you," Karen said, "we have to get back to Portland and then I have to catch a plane to New York. But I really appreciate your offer." She turned to Rachel and gave her a hug. "It was wonderful to see you again. And thanks for the exclusive! Oh, I should warn you, you might have a lot more reporters calling or just showing up here."

Rachel went outside to say goodbye to Karen while the rest of the family headed to their own bedrooms. Crystal put on her pajamas and got in bed, then turned to talk to Taylor.

"Do you really think it was all a miracle, like they were saying?"

"Of course." Taylor said matter-of-factly. "What else could it be? Only God could have done it, so that makes it a miracle."

"Yeah, that makes sense," Crystal agreed.

"Wow, you really are different," Taylor said. "Since when do you think anything I say makes sense?"

"Since you started being sensible," Crystal said.

"School starts next week," Taylor said.

"I know."

"Sister Young is going to take us to get us registered tomorrow or the next day."

"I know."

"Do you think it's going to be weird?"

"I don't know."

"Do you think we will like it here?"

"Yes, I think we will," Crystal assured her.

Taylor turned off the light and Crystal drifted off to sleep. She dreamed of a complete family, of peacefulness and love, and warmth. When she awakened in the morning, she had a smile on her face.

CHAPTER 21

Kenny and Keith practically pulled Crystal and Taylor to the family room as soon as they emerged from their bedroom.

"They keep showing parts of the interview," Keith said, grabbing the remote control.

"And you guys are in the background!" Kenny said.

"Look, here it is again," Keith said.

Crystal watched the interview, focusing her attention on her sister and herself, sitting on the sofa. They didn't look bad. They didn't look strange. They looked like they belonged there. They were part of the family.

The doorbell rang. Crystal heard Sister Young answer it.

"Well, praise God! Look who is here, Dear! Tammy!" she said happily. "You are about the last person I expected to see!"

Crystal shot a panicked look at Taylor and they both ducked behind one of the sofas. This wasn't fair. Tammy could not come and get them. She didn't want them. She couldn't take them away from this home they had finally found. Crystal would not go back to Tennessee with her. She had a family here, who accepted her the way she was, and who loved her.

"Look at you!" Pastor Young was saying. "You are all grown up! I wouldn't have recognized you at all. Praise the Lord!"

Crystal wondered which one of Tammy's kids she had brought with her. It made no difference now. She couldn't have them back. She had given them away, and they weren't even hers.

"Girls, I have a surprise for you," Pastor Young called. They didn't respond.

"Crystal, Taylor, someone is here to see you," Sister Young said. "I thought I heard them out here. Do you boys know where they went?"

Kenny's head popped over the top of the sofa. "You've got company," he said.

Crystal's mind was racing as she tried to think of what to say, how to say no, she wasn't going to go back to Tennessee with Tammy. She and Taylor reluctantly stood up from their hiding place and looked into the face of a complete stranger. This wasn't Tammy... and who was that boy?

Everybody froze as Crystal and Taylor stared at the brown lady and mixed young man who were standing across from them in the family room. Something began to stir inside Crystal... a memory from a long, long time ago.

"Do you know who I am?" the lady asked. The voice... the eyes just like Taylor's eyes... were so familiar, as if from a dream...

"Mommy?" Crystal said, as a tear ran down her cheek. Her mother -- her real mother – reached out to hug her girls. Crystal didn't remember that her name was Tammy.

"Do you remember your brother, Murray?" she asked. So that was Murray, Crystal recalled. She did remember him now.

"I thought--" Crystal began, then couldn't finish her thought.

"I have been looking for you for seven years," her mother said. "I did some things I am not proud of, and I went to jail for three years. My biggest mistake was, after I was in jail, telling your father that I didn't want anything to do with him, and then he took off with you two. You were staying with your grandmother, my mother, in California, and your father came and asked her if he could take you to the park for a couple of hours. Then he never brought you back. As soon as I got out of jail, I hired a private detective to find him, but do you know how many Johnsons there are in the United States? He hadn't even finished searching California. And we didn't know if your father had changed his name.

"I have been praying every night for more than seven years, that God would bring you back to me, or give me a clue as to where you were. Then I saw you on TV last night – I knew it was you, it had to be you, because it just made sense that you would be visiting Pastor and Sister Young. Where is your father, anyway? I have some things I need to straighten out with him."

"Oh, you haven't heard," Sister Young said.

"He killed himself," Taylor announced.

"He what?" Tammy asked, astonished.

"Last January," Crystal added softly.

"Oh, I am so sorry," Tammy said. "I knew he was a good parent, and I was never worried about your welfare... I can't believe it. How could he have done that to you? Oh, thank God, I have finally found you."

They all stood in a big group hug, a family hug, laughing and crying, and they let the phone ring and ring.

Books by Dana Pride

My Friend Is Deaf
Kissing a Dead Man
All These Things

Everlasting Publishing
P.O. Box 1061
Yakima, WA 98907

www.ingramcontent.com/pod-product-compliance
Lightning Source LLC
Chambersburg PA
CBHW060152130626
46556CB00006B/2603